Greek Billionaires

Two billionaire brothers...brides wanted!

Gorgeous Greek brothers Akis and Vannis Giannopoulos have the world at their feet.

They have everything they need...except love.

Until their lives—and hearts!—are turned upside down when two feisty women arrive on their luxurious Greek island...

Akis meets his match, and the only woman who can discover the man beneath the suit and tie, in ***The Millionaire's True Worth***

And look out for

A Wedding for the Greek Tycoon

Available from September 2015

Let Rebecca Winters whisk you away with this riveting and emotional new duet!

Dear Reader,

From the time I was a little girl, I loved the Greek myths, and that love continued to grow as I grew up. In high school my English teacher spent a whole semester on the myths, and we had to learn a lot of the terminology.

When I began writing, I found that a lot of the myths we'd studied came to my mind. They are wonderful stories with different twists, much like the twists in the love stories of a Harlequin Romance story. In writing this duet about Greek Billionaires, my mind automatically imagined them living on one of the gorgeous Greek Islands. Of course, living by the water, they swim like fish.

Suddenly I remembered some of the myths of the God of the Water, Poseidon. One of the stories about him took hold of me, and I wrote this first story, *The Millionaire's True Worth*. Everything seemed to fit with the plot I had devised. I hope when you read this story, you'll be intrigued enough to read a few Greek myths on your own. They're wonderful!

Enjoy!

Rebecca Winters

The Millionaire's True Worth

—

Rebecca Winters

(H) HARLEQUIN®ROMANCE

Recycling programs
for this product may
not exist in your area.

ISBN-13: 978-0-373-74345-2

The Millionaire's True Worth

First North American Publication 2015

Copyright © 2015 by Rebecca Winters

All rights reserved. Except for use in any review, the reproduction or
utilization of this work in whole or in part in any form by any electronic,
mechanical or other means, now known or hereinafter invented, including
xerography, photocopying and recording, or in any information storage
or retrieval system, is forbidden without the written permission of the
publisher, Harlequin Enterprises Limited, 225 Duncan Mill Road,
Don Mills, Ontario M3B 3K9, Canada.

This is a work of fiction. Names, characters, places and incidents are
either the product of the author's imagination or are used fictitiously,
and any resemblance to actual persons, living or dead, business
establishments, events or locales is entirely coincidental.

This edition published by arrangement with Harlequin Books S.A.

For questions and comments about the quality of this book,
please contact us at CustomerService@Harlequin.com.

® and TM are trademarks of Harlequin Enterprises Limited or its
corporate affiliates. Trademarks indicated with ® are registered in the
United States Patent and Trademark Office, the Canadian Intellectual
Property Office and in other countries.

Printed in U.S.A.

www.Harlequin.com

Rebecca Winters lives in Salt Lake City, Utah. With canyons and high alpine meadows full of wildflowers, she never runs out of places to explore. They, plus her favorite vacation spots in Europe, often end up as backgrounds for her romance novels, because writing is her passion, along with her family and church.

Rebecca loves to hear from readers. If you wish to email her, please visit her website at cleanromances.com.

Books by Rebecca Winters

HARLEQUIN® ROMANCE

Princes of Europe

Expecting the Prince's Baby
Becoming the Prince's Wife

Gingerbread Girls

Marry Me under the Mistletoe

Tiny Miracles

Baby Out of the Blue
Along Came Twins...

The Count's Christmas Baby
A Marriage Made in Italy
The Greek's Tiny Miracle
At the Chateau for Christmas
Taming the French Tycoon
The Renegade Billionaire

Visit the author profile page
at Harlequin.com for more titles

CHAPTER ONE

"CHLOE? I'M SORRY I can't be your maid of honor, but you know why."

Following that statement there was a long silence on Chloe's part. But Raina had her job plus the many responsibilities thrown onto her shoulders since the death of her grandfather. She was now heiress to the Maywood billion-dollar fortune and was constantly in the news. When she went out in public, the paparazzi were right on her heels.

Chloe's family were high-profile Greek industrialists, a favorite target of the European paparazzi. Her marriage would be the top story in Athens. "If I were your maid of honor, the media would make a circus out of your special day." Raina feared it would take the spotlight off her dear friend. For Chloe's sake, she couldn't risk it.

Too much had happened in the intervening

years. It had been eight years, in fact, since Chloe had lived with Raina and her grandparents during her senior year of high school. But they'd stayed in touch by phone and the internet.

Three years ago Raina's grandmother had died and Chloe had come to California with her parents for the funeral. Just nine months ago Raina's grandfather had died and once again Chloe and her family had flown over to be with her for his funeral. Their close friendship had helped her get through her grief, and Chloe's family had begged Raina to come back to Greece with them.

"Please tell me you understand, Chloe. I have no desire to intrude on your joy."

"I don't care about me."

"But I *do*."

After a resigned sigh Chloe said, "Then at least stay at the house with me and my family. After all you did for me when I lived with you, my parents are anxious to do everything they can for you."

"Tell you what. After you've left on your honeymoon I'll be thrilled to spend time with them before I fly back to California."

"They'll want you to stay for several months.

Think about it. We could have such a wonderful time together."

"I will think about it. As for right now I can't wait to be at your reception. The photos you sent me in your wedding dress are fabulous!"

"But you won't get to see me married at the church."

"Much as I'm sorry about that, it's better this way. I've already booked a room at the Diethnes Hotel. You can reach me on the phone there or on my cell phone. Chloe? You promise you haven't told your fiancé my plans?"

"I swear it. Of course he knows all about you, but he doesn't have any idea that you are coming to Greece."

"Good. That's how I want things to stay. This is going to be *your* day! If the press finds out I'm there, I'm afraid it will ruin things for you. Later this year I'll fly over to meet him, or you can fly to California."

"I promise. He's so wonderful, I can't eat or sleep."

"That doesn't surprise me. *Ta le-me*, Chloe," she said, using one of the few Greek expressions she still remembered, before hanging up.

Six years ago Raina had been in the same

excited condition as her friend. Halfway through college she'd met Byron Wallace, a writer. After a whirlwind romance they were married. But it didn't take long to see his selfish nature and suspect her new husband of being unfaithful. Armed with proof of his infidelity even before their two-year marriage anniversary, she'd divorced him, only to lose her grandmother to heart failure.

In her pain she vowed never to marry again. She'd told as much to her beloved, ailing grandfather who'd passed away from stomach cancer.

Chloe's phone call a month ago about her impending marriage had come as a wonderful surprise. Since the death of Raina's grandfather, it was the one piece of news that put some excitement back into her life.

The head of her team at the lab was aware she hadn't taken a vacation in several years. He urged her to take the time off for as long as she wanted. "Go to Greece and be with your friend," he'd said. "We'll still be here when you get back."

Raina thought about it. A change of scene to enjoy Chloe's nuptials might be exactly what she needed.

* * *

Maybe it was the stress of everything she'd had to do before her flight to Athens, Greece. All Raina knew was that she had developed a splitting headache. She needed a strong pain-killer. After filing out of the coach section to clear customs wearing jeans and a T-shirt, she retrieved her medium-sized suitcase and left the terminal late morning to find a taxi.

"The Diethnes Hotel, please," she told the driver. The man at the travel agency in Carmel-by-the-Sea, California, had booked the budget hotel for her. From there she could walk to Syntagma Square and the city center without problem.

Chloe had phoned her from Athens yes-terday to exclaim over the gorgeous seventy-eight-degree temperature, perfect for her June wedding that would take place tomorrow. Considering the prominence of the Milonis and Chiotis families, it promised to be one of the country's major society events of the summer.

Raina, a strawberry blonde with wavy hair cut neck length, looked at the clear blue Greek sky, a good omen for the impending festivities. Chloe was the sweetest girl in the world. Raina hoped she was marrying an honorable man who'd be true to her.

Raina hadn't been so lucky in that department, but four years had passed since the divorce and she refused to let any remaining clouds dampen the excitement for her friend. Every woman went into marriage praying it would last forever. *A woman had that right, didn't she?*

Once she'd been shown to her room and had unpacked, Raina went back downstairs for directions to the nearest pharmacy for headache medicine. The concierge told her there was a convenience store in the next block many of the American tourists frequented.

Raina thanked him and made her way down the street.

Akis Giannopoulos smiled at his best friend. "Are you ready to take the big plunge?"

Theo grinned. "You already know the answer to that question. If I'd had my way, I would have kidnapped Chloe and married her in private several months ago. But her mother and mine have had an agenda since the engagement. Wouldn't you know the guest list includes a cast of thousands?"

"You're a lucky man." Akis was happy for him. Theo and Chloe seemed to be a perfect match. "Can I do any last-minute service for you before you become a married man?"

"You did more than enough helping me make all the hotel arrangements for our out-of-town guests. I suggest you go back to the penthouse. I need my best man relaxed before the big day tomorrow. Will your brother be there?"

"Vasso phoned me earlier. He'll make it to the wedding, but then he has to get back to the grand opening so he'll miss the reception."

"Understood. So, I'll see you at the church in the morning?"

Akis hugged him. "Try to keep me away."

The two men had been friends for a long time. Naturally Akis was thrilled for Theo, but he was surprised to discover just how much he would miss the camaraderie they'd shared as bachelors. Having done so many things together, Akis was feeling a real sense of loss.

Theo's life would now be swept up with Chloe's. Falling in love with her had changed his friend. He was excited for this marriage. Akis marveled that Theo wanted it so much.

How could he feel so certain that marrying Chloe was the right thing for him?

Marriage meant a lifelong commitment. The woman would have to be so sensational. Akis couldn't fathom finding such a woman.

Aware he was in a despondent mood that wasn't like him, he left the bank Theo's family had owned for several decades and decided to walk to the penthouse in order to shake it off. After the wedding rehearsal that had taken place this morning, exercise was what he needed.

Tourists had flooded into Athens. He saw every kind and description as he made his way to the Giannopoulos complex. After turning a corner, he almost bumped into a beautiful female in a T-shirt and jeans coming in his direction.

"Me seen xo rees, thespinis," he apologized, getting out of her way just in time.

She murmured something he didn't quite hear. For a moment their eyes locked. He felt like he'd suddenly come in contact with an electric current. She must have felt it, too, because he saw little bursts of violet coming from those velvety depths before she walked on. By the way she moved, she had a definite destination in mind. The last thing he saw was her blondish-red hair gleaming in the sun before she rounded the corner behind him.

Raina slowed down, shocked by what had just happened. Maybe it was her bad headache that had caused her to almost walk into the most gorgeous male she'd ever seen in her life. Not in her wildest dreams could she have conjured such a man.

She needed medicine fast!

Luckily the sign for the convenience store was in Greek and English. Alpha/Omega 24. Translation—everything from A to Z. That was a clever name for the store. Its interior looked like "everywhere USA." There was a caution sign saying Wet Floor in both languages as you walked in.

She tiptoed over the newly mopped floor in her sandals to the counter. The male clerk, probably college age, helped her find the over-the-counter medicine section for headaches.

After picking it out plus a bottle of water, she followed him back to the counter to pay for the items with some euros. While she waited, she opened the water and took two pills. On her way out, the clerk asked her where she was staying. Raina told him she was just passing through and started for the exit. But somehow, she didn't know how, she slipped and fell.

"Whoa—" Pain radiated from her ankle. The clerk rushed from behind the counter to help her get up. When she tried to stand, it really hurt. Hopefully the medicine would help tamp down the pain.

He hurried into a back room and brought out a chair so she could sit down. "I'm calling the hospital."

"I don't think there's a need for that."

He ignored her. "This is the store's fault. You stay there."

She felt the fool sitting there while there were customers coming in and out. The other clerk who'd mopped the floor waited on them. In a few minutes an ambulance drove up in front. By then she'd answered a few questions the clerk had asked in order to fill out an incident form.

Because she was incognito, she gave her grandmother's name with her information so no one would pick up on her name. To her dismay there was a small crowd standing around as she was helped outside. Great! Exactly what she didn't want.

"Thank you," she said to the clerk before being helped into the back by one of the attendants. "You've been very kind and I appreciate it."

Two hours later her sprain had been wrapped. She needed to put ice on it and elevate her leg to cut down the swelling. The ER doctor fitted her with crutches and sent them with her in the taxi, letting her know the bill would be taken care of by the store where she'd fallen.

After the wedding reception, Raina would make certain her insurance company would reimburse the store. After all, the accident was her fault.

For the time being, she needed to lie down and call room service for her meals and ice. How crazy was it that she would have to go to the reception tomorrow evening on crutches. No matter what, she refused to miss her dear friend's celebration.

After flying all this way, how even crazier was it that all she could think about was the man she'd come close to colliding with earlier in the day. She'd never experienced anything like that before. The streets of Athens were crowded with hundreds of people. How was it that one man could rob her of breath just looking at him?

With a champagne glass in hand, Akis stood at the head table to toast the bride and groom. "It was a great honor Theo Chiotis bestowed on me when he asked me to be his best man. No man has had a better friend." Except for Vasso, of course. "After meeting and getting to know Chloe, I can say without reservation that no man could have married a sweeter woman. To Theo and Chloe. May you always be as happy as you are today."

After the crowd applauded, other friends of the bridal couple made their toasts. Akis was thankful his part in the long wedding-day festivities was officially over. When he felt a decent interval of time had passed, he would slip out of the luxurious Grand Bretagne Hotel ballroom unnoticed and leave for the penthouse.

To love a woman enough to go through this exhaustive kind of day was anathema to Akis. No man appreciated women more than he did, but his business affairs with thirty-year-old Vasso kept him too busy to enjoy more than a surface relationship that didn't last long.

Though he congratulated himself on reaching the age of twenty-nine without yet succumbing to marriage, Theo's wedding caused Akis to question what was going on with him and his brother.

The two of them had been in business since they were young boys. To this point in time no enduring love interest had interfered with their lives and they'd managed to make their dream to rise out of poverty come true. Besides owning a conglomerate of retail stores throughout Greece, they'd set up a charity Foundation with two centers, one in Greece, the other in New York City.

Their dirt-poor background might be a memory, but it was the one that drove them so they'd never know what it was like to go hungry again. Unfortunately their ascent from rags to riches didn't come without some drawbacks. For various reasons both he and Vasso found it difficult to trust the women who came into their lives. They enjoyed brief relationships. But they grew leery when they came across women who seemed to love them for themselves, with no interest in their money. He thought about their parents who, though they were painfully poor and scraped for every drachma, had loved and were devoted to one another. They came from the same island with the same expectations of life and the ability to endure the ups and downs of marriage. Both Akis and Vasso wanted a union like their parents', one that would last forever. But finding the right woman seemed to be growing harder.

Akis's thoughts wandered back to the words he'd just spoken to the guests in the ballroom. He'd meant what he'd said about Chloe, who was kind and compatible. She suited Theo, who also had a winning nature. They both came from the same elite, socioeconomic background that helped them to trust that neither had an agenda. If two people could make it through this life together and be happy, he imagined they would.

Every so often he felt the maid of honor's dark eyes willing him to pay attention to her. Althea Loris was one of Chloe's friends, a very glamorous woman as yet unattached. She'd tried to corner him at various parties given before the wedding. Althea came from a good family with a modest income, but Akis sensed how much she wanted all the trappings of a marriage like Chloe's.

Even if Akis had felt an attraction, he would have wondered if she'd set her eyes on him for what he could give her monetarily. It wasn't fair to judge, but he couldn't ignore his basic instinct about her.

There was nothing he wanted more than to be loved for himself. An imperfect self, to be sure. Both he and Vasso had been born into a family where you worked by the sweat of your brow all the days of your life. The idea of a formal education was unheard of, but he hadn't worried about it until the summer right before he had to do his military service.

An Italian tourist named Fabrizia, who was staying on the island that July, had flirted with Akis at the store where he worked. He couldn't speak Italian, nor she Greek, so they managed with passable English. He was attracted and spent time swimming with her when he could get an hour off. By the time she had to go home, he'd fallen for her and wanted to know when she'd be back.

After kissing him passionately she'd said, "I won't be able to come." In the next breath she'd told him she'd be getting married soon to one of the attorneys working for her father in Rome. "But I'll never forget my beautiful grocery boy. Why couldn't you be the attorney my parents have picked out for me?"

Not only had his pride taken a direct hit, her question had made him startlingly aware of his shortcomings, the kind that went soil-deep. The kind that separated the rich from the poor. From that time on, Akis had enjoyed several relationships with women, but they didn't approach the level of his wanting to get married.

Too bad his brother had to leave after the wedding at the church and couldn't attend the reception. He was away on important business at the moment so he couldn't rescue Akis with a legitimate excuse to leave early. Akis would have to manufacture a good one on his own.

Thankfully the speeches were almost over. Chloe's father was the last person to speak. After getting choked up because he was losing his precious daughter to Theo, he urged everyone to enjoy the rest of the evening and dance.

Akis watched as Theo escorted Chloe to

the floor for the first dance. Soon other couples joined them. That meant Akis had to fulfill one last duty. It was expected that he ask Althea, who was more than eager to find herself in his arms.

"I've been waiting for this all day, Akis."

He knew what she was saying, what she was hoping for, but he couldn't force interest that wasn't there. The long, exhausting wedding day was almost over. Akis couldn't wait to leave, but he needed to choose his words carefully. "Unfortunately I still have business to do after the reception is over."

Her head jerked up. "Business? Tonight?"

"My work is never done." As the music was coming to an end, he danced her over to her parents' table and let her go. "Thank you, Althea. Theo asked me to mingle so if you'll excuse me, there's one more person I should dance with before I leave." The lie had just come to him.

While she looked at him with genuine disappointment, he smiled at her parents before he moved through the crowded room toward the rear of the ballroom. In order to prove he hadn't told an untruth, he looked for any woman at one of the tables who didn't have an escort, whom he could ask to dance.

At the round table nearest the rear doors he saw a woman sitting alone. Another couple sat across from her, but it was clear she didn't have a man with her. Knowing Althea was still watching him, he walked toward the stranger. Maybe she was waiting for someone, but he'd take his chances.

Closer now he could make out classic features beneath hair an incredible light gold with a natural hint of red. He'd only seen hair that color on one other woman. His breath caught. She wore a pale blue silk suit jacket with a small enamel locket hanging around her neck. He imagined she was in her mid-twenties. He saw no rings.

Akis approached her. "Excuse me, *thespinis*. I see you're alone for the moment. As best man of this wedding, if you'd permit, I'd like to dance with you."

Her eyes lifted to his.

Those eyes. They were the same eyes he'd looked into yesterday, but tonight he discovered they were a stunning shade of lavender blue and he found himself lost in them.

"I'm sorry, but I don't speak Greek."

Her comment jarred him back to the present. What was this American beauty doing at Theo's wedding reception? Switching to unpolished English he said, "We passed in the street yesterday."

"I remember almost bumping into you," she murmured, averting her eyes. He noticed with satisfaction that a nerve throbbed in her throat above her locket. She was as excited as he was by this unexpected meeting. "I came close to knocking you down because I wasn't watching where I was going."

He smiled. "No problem. Just now I asked you to dance, but perhaps you're waiting for the man who brought you."

A delicate flush filled her cheeks. "No. I came alone. Thank you for the invitation, but I was just getting ready to leave."

He wasn't about to let her go a second time. "Surely you can spare one dance with me? I need rescuing."

"Where's your wife?"

"I've never had a wife. As for a girlfriend, I haven't had one in months." It was the truth.

"Then who was the woman with the long black hair you were dancing with moments ago?"

So she'd noticed. "You're very observant. She was the maid of honor. It would have been unkind not to dance with her."

With a twinkle in her eyes, she leaned to the right and retrieved a pair of crutches from the floor. She stood them on end. "Unless you're prepared for your feet to be impaled by one of these, I'll do you a favor and exit the room."

She'd surprised Akis. This had to be a very recent injury. Her legitimate excuse to turn him down only fed his determination to get to know her better. Yesterday he'd wanted to pursue her, but hadn't dared for fear of alarming her. "Then let me help you."

Without hesitation he took the crutches from her and waited until she got to her feet. She was probably five foot seven, with enticing curves. The matching suit skirt covered womanly hips and slender legs. His gaze fell lower to the left ankle that had been wrapped. She wore a sandal on her foot and a low-heeled shoe on the other.

"Thank you." She reached for the crutches and fit them beneath her arms. The delicate fragrance emanating from her assailed him. "Why don't you ask the other woman at my table to dance? I'm sure her partner won't mind."

"I'd rather help you to your room."

"I'm not staying here."

That was interesting. He'd helped Theo make arrangements for all their out-of-town guests to stay here. "Then I'll walk you outside and take you wherever you'd like to go."

"As long as you're offering, I wouldn't say no if you hailed a taxi for me. I'm craving my hotel room so I can elevate my leg."

"I'll do better than that." Akis accompanied her from the ballroom and down the hall to the foyer. The woman at his side managed her crutches with little trouble. En route he phoned his driver and told him to come to the hotel entrance.

As they walked outside, flashes from the cameras of the paparazzi blinded them. Chloe and Theo's wedding would be the top story making the ten o'clock news on television. Video of prominent guests and the best man attending the reception filmed by TV news crews would be included.

Some of the paparazzi called out questions about the beautiful woman with Akis. He hated the attention though he was used to it, and kept walking her to the smoked-glass limo without answering them. He took her crutches so she could get in, then he followed and shut the door before sitting opposite her. "Are you all right?"

"I am. Are you?"

"I am now. The press is unrelenting. Tell me where you're staying and I'll let the driver know."

"The Diethnes."

A lot of tourists on a budget frequented two-star hotels like that one. Until he and Vasso had started making money, he could never have afforded to stay at any hotel. Period. Akis gave his driver directions and they pulled away from the Grand Bretagne. "When did you have time to injure your ankle?"

She let out a sound of exasperation. "It happened right after you and I passed on the sidewalk. I had a headache and was on my way to a store for some medicine. While I was inside, I slipped on the wet floor. It was such a stupid accident, totally my fault for not paying attention. The clerk was incredibly kind and called the ambulance for me."

Akis mulled over her answer. Had she decided it would be easier to attend the reception rather than the wedding because of her injury? If she'd been at the church, he wouldn't have been able to take his eyes off her during the ceremony.

"Are you in pain?"

"Not really. It's more a dull ache until I rest it."

"I'm sorry you had to fall, especially the day before the wedding."

"Funny about life, isn't it?" she murmured. "You never know what's going to happen when you get up in the morning." The almost haunted tone in her voice intrigued him.

"How true. When I left for the wedding, I didn't know I was going to meet the lovely stranger who'd passed me on the street yesterday."

"Or be chased by the maid of honor tonight," she said in a wry tone. "Am I mistaken, or were you taking flight?"

"You noticed that."

"It was hard not to." She chuckled without looking at him. "I would imagine a man with your looks and minus a wedding ring needs rescuing from myriads of females."

He blinked. "*My* looks?"

"You know very well you're the embodiment of a Greek god."

Akis frowned. "Which terrifying one are you referring to?"

At this point she laughed. "I didn't have any particular god in mind. It's something American women say when they've met an exceptionally good-looking man."

"Then they haven't seen one of our Greek statues up close or they'd run for their lives in the other direction."

Her laughing continued. He decided she was somewhat of a tease.

"I don't know. Despite your fearsome expression, the female pursuing you tonight didn't seem turned off by you. Quite the opposite, in fact."

That's exactly what Althea had been doing for weeks. Maybe he'd misjudged her, but it didn't matter because he hadn't been attracted. "You saved me from being caught. For that, I'm in your debt."

"I'm in yours for giving me a lift to the hotel," she came right back. "We're even."

Akis had never met a woman like her. "Are you a friend of Theo's or Chloe's? I don't even know your name."

"Let's keep it that way."

Her remark shouldn't have bothered him, but it did...

They continued down the busy street. "Oh— Look—" she cried softly. "See that store on the right? Alpha/Omega 24?" He nodded. "That's the one where I fell. My hotel is in the next block."

Raina couldn't believe that the incredible man she'd seen on the street yesterday was none other than Theo's best man. It was an amazing coincidence. She was actually upset with herself for having any feelings about seeing him again tonight.

Since her divorce, there'd been no man in her life and she'd purposely kept it that way. She didn't want to fall in love again and take the chance of being hurt. For this man to have already made an impact on her without even trying was disturbing. After the pain she'd been through because of Byron, she never wanted to experience it again.

When the driver drove up in front of the hotel, Raina was relieved that the striking Greek male sitting next to her had gone quiet and didn't pressure her for more information. That was good.

She found that when she used a man's tactics of a little false flattery on him, the fun went out of it on his part. Knowing Raina could see through his strategy, his interest had quickly waned. She wanted to leave Greece with no complications. Already she knew this man was unforgettable. The sooner she could get away from him, the better.

"Thanks again for the lift," she said in a cheery voice, needing to escape the potency of his male charisma.

He opened the door and took her crutches to help her from the back of the limo. She put them underneath her arms and started for the entrance. After pushing the hotel door open, he accompanied her as far as the foyer. She kept moving toward the elevator. While she waited, she turned in his direction.

"Like you, I appreciated being rescued." The lift door finally opened. "Good night." She stepped inside without looking back, praying for it to close fast in case he decided to go upstairs with her.

Raina willed her heart to stop thudding. She hadn't been kidding when she'd said he

looked like a Greek god. From his black hair
and eyes to his tall, powerful build, he was
the personification of male perfection. She
hadn't been able to take her eyes off him all
evening. His image would be all over the television tonight, causing legions of women to
swoon.

Chloe had raved about Theo's looks, but he
couldn't hold a candle to his best man. What
had she called him? Akis something or other.
He had a self-assured presence, bordering on
an arrogance he probably wasn't aware of.

The maid of honor who'd danced with him
earlier had looked pained when he'd left her
side and made a beeline to Raina's table. Here
Raina had tried so hard to be invisible during the reception. But at least no one recognized her.

So far the only photos taken of her were
because the best man with his Greek-god
looks had helped her out to the limo. Until
now Raina had managed to escape any notoriety. The paparazzi were following him,
not her. Chloe's beautiful day had gone per-
fectly without a marring incident of any kind.
If ever a bride looked euphoric...

Grateful for the reception to be over, she let

herself into the room. To her surprise there was a light blinking on the phone. It couldn't possibly be Chloe. Maybe it was the front desk. She used her crutches to reach the bedside and sat down to find out if something was wrong.

When she picked up, she listened to the message from Nora Milonis, Chloe's mother. She was sending a car for Raina in the morning and insisted she spend the rest of her time in Athens with them. *Be ready at 9:00 a.m.* Absolutely no excuses now that the wedding was over!

She'd known the invitation was coming. It warmed her heart and put her in a much better mood.

Once she'd called for ice and was ready for bed, she elevated her leg and turned on the TV. But her mind wandered to the man who'd brought her home.

He spoke English with a deep, heavy Greek accent she found appealing. The man hadn't done anything, yet he'd disturbed her senses that had lain dormant since she'd discovered her husband had been unfaithful to her. The way he'd looked at her both yesterday and tonight had made her feel alive for the first time in years and he hadn't even touched her!

Why this man? Why now? She couldn't understand what it was that made him so fascinating to her. That was the trouble. She didn't want to find him fascinating because it meant a part of her wanted to see him again.

She'd planned to fly back to California soon, but her sprained ankle prevented her from leaving for a while. How wonderful that she'd be able to spend time with Chloe's parents after all! Raina needed family right now, even if it wasn't her own.

The doctor had warned her to keep it supported close to a week for a faster recovery. She'd planned to do work on her laptop and get in some reading.

Anything to keep her mind off Theo's best man.

CHAPTER TWO

"*KALIMERA*, GALEN."

The clerk's head lifted. "Kyrie Giannopoulos—what a surprise to see you in here this morning! I didn't expect a visit before next week."

Galen reminded Akis of himself at an earlier age. He was eager for the work and anxious to please. So far, Akis had had no complaints about him. "I came by to find out if you were on duty the day before yesterday when an American woman slipped and fell."

"Yes. Mikos and I were both here. How did you know?"

"That's not important. Tell me what happened."

Akis listened as his employee recounted the same story the exciting woman had told him last night. "Did she threaten to sue?"

"No. She claimed it was her fault."

"Did you fill out an incident report?"

"Yes. It's on the desk in the back room. I told the ambulance attendant the store would be responsible for the bill."

"You did exactly the right thing. Thank you."

Akis walked behind the counter and entered the small room, anxious to see what was written. He reached in the Out basket and found the injury report.

June 3, 1:45 p.m.
Ginger Moss: American, age 26
Athens address: The Diethnes Hotel.
Customer fell on wet floor after purchasing some headache medicine. She limped in pain. I called an ambulance. She was taken to St. Michael's Hospital. Signed: Galen.

Ginger... He liked the name very much. He liked everything about her *too* much. She'd caused him a restless night despite the fact that the whole wedding day had been exhausting. Ginger Moss had that effect on a man.

Akis had felt her magic and couldn't throw it off. Now that he was armed with her name, he planned to seek her out so he could get to know her better. Since he didn't know her agenda, he had no idea how long she'd be in Athens. The only way to find out was to head over to her hotel.

Galen poked his head in the door. "Is everything all right, boss?"

"You two are doing a fine job."

"Thanks. About that American woman who slipped and fell?"

Akis turned his head to look at his employee. "Yes?"

"Mikos had just mopped the floor before she came in. We did have the caution sign set out on the floor."

"Good." He nodded to his two employees and went back out to the limo. "I'll walk to the Diethnes from here," he told the driver. "Follow me and wait in front until you hear from me again."

A few minutes later he entered the hotel lobby and told the concierge he'd like to speak to one of their guests named Ginger Moss. The other man shook his head. "We don't have a tourist staying here with that name."

Akis unconsciously ran a hand through his hair in surprise. "You're sure? Maybe if I explain that the woman I'm looking for was using crutches when I dropped her off here last night."

"Ah… The one with hair the color of a Titian painting and a figure like the statue in the museum. You know—the one of the goddess Aphrodite carrying a pitcher?"

Yes—that was the precise one Akis had envisioned himself.

He thought back to last night. She'd been elusive about everything. What kind of a game was she playing? He closed his eyes tightly for a moment, remembering her comment about him resembling a Greek god. *Touché.*

"Would you ring her room and tell her the man who helped her home last night is in the lobby and wishes to talk to her?"

His shoulders hunched. "I can't. She checked out an hour ago."

"You mean permanently?" he barked the question.

"Of course."

"Did she leave a forwarding address?"

"No. I'm sorry."

"Did she go by taxi?"

"I don't know. I was busy at the desk."

"What name did she register under?"

"Unless you have a judge's warrant, I can't tell you."

Trying to tamp down his frustration, he thanked the man and hurried outside to the limo where his driver was waiting.

"Shall I take you to the office?

"Not yet. I have a phone call to make first." Akis climbed in the back and phoned Theo's parents. He reached his friend's mother. After chatting for a moment about the perfect wedding, she mentioned Althea and her disappointment that Akis had needed to leave the reception so soon. Akis reminded her that something pressing in business had come up. Then he got to the point.

"Did you invite an American woman named Ginger Moss to the wedding reception?"

"Moss? No," she claimed after reflection. "That's an unusual name, and it certainly wasn't on our list or I would have remembered. Why?"

So that was the reason why Theo hadn't arranged for her to stay at the Grand Bretagne. "I'm trying to find her."

After a silence, "Is she the person who caused you to walk away from Althea so fast last night?"

Akis didn't mind her teasing insinuation. Theo's parents were like a second family to him. For the last year both of them had kept reminding him it was time he got married, too. "No. As I was leaving the ballroom, I ran into the woman who was on crutches and needed help out to a taxi."

"Hmm. Why don't you check with Chloe's parents? They must have invited her. If they haven't heard of her, either, maybe she was a friend of Chloe's or Theo's. Perhaps they invited her too late to receive an invitation."

"Maybe," he muttered. "She hadn't been at the church or *I* would have remembered," he said quietly. "Thanks. We'll all have to get together after they get back from their honeymoon."

"Wonderful, but don't you dare be a stranger while they're away!"

"I won't," Akis promised, but his mind was on the woman he'd asked to dance last night. He could have sworn there'd been feelings between them. Sparks. Some nuance of chemistry that had happened immediately while they were on the sidewalk and wouldn't leave him alone. Yet she'd run off this morning.

No matter what, he intended to find her.

It bothered him that she'd given him the slip when she knew he wanted to get to know her better. Maybe it was his pride that made him want to prove she had feelings for him, too. One thing was certain. He wasn't going to let her disappear on him.

Without wasting another moment, he phoned Chloe's house. The housekeeper said she'd put through the call to Chloe's father because Kyria Milonis was occupied.

The more Akis thought about it, the more he decided this woman had to be a friend of Chloe's. Otherwise Theo would have talked about her long before now. He wouldn't have been able to help himself because even if he was head over heels in love with Chloe, this Ginger, or whoever she was, stood out from the rest.

Why had she sat at the last table near the doors last night? It was almost as if she hadn't wanted to be seen. Her behavior was a mystery to him. Vasso would be shocked by the strength of his brother's desire to find the tantalizing female. Nothing like this had ever happened before. No one was more shocked than Akis himself. In case she'd be leaving Athens soon, he had to work fast.

"Akis, my boy!" came the booming voice of Chloe's father. "Great to hear from you! We're going to miss the kids. The place feels empty. Come on over to the house for lunch. My wife will be thrilled. We'll eat by the pool."

The perfect place to vet Chloe's parents. "I'll be there soon, Socus. Thank you."

After getting settled on a patio lounger by the pool with her leg raised, Raina smiled at Chloe's mother who hovered around her like her grandmother used to do. She loved her friend's parents and drew great comfort from being with them. They couldn't seem to do enough for her.

"We were always sorry that you didn't come to live with us after Chloe's school year with you ended. It was all Chloe had talked about."

"I would have come, but as you know my grandmother wasn't well and I was afraid to leave her. Then I started college and met the man who became my husband. When our marriage didn't work out, I divorced him. Then, of course, my grandmother died and I needed to take care of my grandfather, who was diagnosed with stomach cancer. There was never a good time to come to Greece."

Chloe's father patted her hand. "You've had a great load on your shoulders."

"My grandparents raised me. I loved them so much and owed them everything. But I have to tell you, the year Chloe spent with me was the happiest of my life. It was like having a sister. My grandparents adored her."

Nora smiled with tears in her eyes. "She loved the three of you. Why don't you consider this your temporary home and stay with us for a time? There's nothing we'd like more. Chloe would be ecstatic."

"That would be wonderful, but I have a job waiting for me when I get back."

"You like your work?"

"Very much," but she was prevented from saying more because a maid appeared beneath the striped patio awning. She said something in Greek and suddenly the best man walked out on the terrace.

"Akis!" Nora cried with warmth in her voice.

Raina's heart skipped several beats. In a short-sleeved white crew neck and matching cargo pants, he robbed her of breath, with his rock-hard physique and arresting Greek features.

He hadn't seen Raina yet and said something in Greek to Chloe's parents with an aura of authority she was sure came naturally to him. He sounded intense, with no accompanying smile. After he stopped talking, they both started to chuckle and turned to Raina.

The man's dark head jerked around in her direction. His penetrating gaze caused her body to fill with heat. To her dismay she lay helpless on the lounger in another T-shirt and jeans with her leg propped, hardly an exciting sight. The look of shock on his face was priceless.

"You're here," he muttered, rubbing his chest absently. "I went to the hotel but the concierge said you'd already checked out. Theo's parents claimed they didn't know you, so I decided to come over here to find out if you were a friend of Chloe's."

The knowledge that he'd been trying to find her excited her. Again she was struck by his heavily accented English. For want of a better word, she found it endearing. Raina nodded to him, stunned that he'd gone to such lengths to find her. "Friends from a long time ago. Her parents sent a car for me this morning so we could visit."

"Which has been long overdue," Nora stated in English.

He still looked thunderstruck. Raina could read his mind. "Did you think I had invited myself to the reception?"

"No, but I got the feeling you didn't want to be noticed," he drawled. She had the feeling nothing got past him.

"While you two talk, I'll tell Ione to serve lunch out here." Nora got up from the deck chair and Chloe's father followed her, leaving them alone.

Raina swallowed hard. She never imagined seeing him again and wasn't prepared for this overwhelming response to the very sight of him.

He pulled up a deck chair and sat down next to her. His black eyes played over her from head to toe, missing nothing in between. Her pulse raced. "How's the pain this morning?"

"I took an ibuprofen and now it's hardly noticeable. At this rate I'll be able to fly home soon."

"What's the rush?"

"Work is waiting for me." *I don't dare spend*

any more time around you. I didn't come to Greece to meet a man who has already become too important to me.

He leaned forward with his hands clasped between his hard muscled legs. "What kind?"

Oh, boy. She could tell she was in for a vetting. The less he knew about her, the better. She was afraid to be open with her feelings for fear of being hurt again. After having made a huge mistake in choosing Byron, she feared she didn't have wise judgment when it came to men.

Byron had been relentless in his pursuit of her. She'd been so naive and so flattered by his attention, she'd fallen into his grasping, narcissistic hands like an apple from a tree. His betrayal of her even before their marriage had scarred her for life, forcing her to grow up overnight.

Never again would she allow herself to be caught off guard, even if this man thrilled her to the core of her being. Raina would rather leave Greece without feeling any tug of emotion for this dark-haired stranger. He was already dangerous to her peace of mind.

"I work in a lab with a team of people."

That was as much as she was willing to reveal. "What do you do for a living?"

He studied her intently. "My brother and I are in business. That's how I met Theo. So now that we have that out of the way, how did you meet Chloe?"

Raina could tell he was equally reticent to talk about himself. That was fine with her. He could keep his secrets, whatever they were. "My senior year of high school, she came to live with me in California for the school year so she could learn English. That year there were three other students from other countries living with some of the students' families."

"Was it a reciprocal arrangement?"

"Yes. After graduation I was supposed to spend the next year with her family, but too many things at the time prevented me from coming here to live with them."

Needing some space to gather her composure before he asked her any more questions, she sat up and swung her legs to the ground. He anticipated her movements and handed her the crutches lying by the side of the lounger. "Thank you," she said, tucking them beneath her arms. "If you'll excuse me, please, I need to use the restroom."

"Of course."

Raina could see in his eyes she hadn't fooled him, but what did it matter. She hurried through the mansion to her suite of rooms. The fabulous Milonis estate had been built along neoclassical lines in its purest architectural form. So different from the home where she'd been raised in Carmel.

When she eventually returned to the patio, she discovered Akis in the swimming pool. Their lunch had been brought out to the patio table. While he was doing laps at tremendous speed, she sat down in one of the chairs around the table and dug into the salad filled with delicious chicken, feta cheese and olives.

Chloe's parents were nowhere in sight. Raina had hoped they'd come out to provide a buffer against his questions, but no such luck. Chloe's parents were a very hip couple she adored. Raina could see why. Too bad they thought they were aiding a romantic situation by staying away.

As her eyes looked out at the pool, Akis suddenly raised his head. The wet black hair was swept back from his forehead to reveal

his extraordinary male features. The moment
he saw her, he levered himself from the aquamarine water and reached for a towel, giving her more than a glimpse of his splendid
body. He must have borrowed someone's
black trunks. They hung low on his hips.

"Last night you resembled one of your dis-
gruntled gods," she teased to fight her attraction. "Today you've morphed into Poseidon."

Akis finished drying himself off before he
sat down in a chair opposite her and plucked
a big olive from the salad his white teeth bit
into with relish. Between his olive skin and
black hair, he was a work of art if there was
such a label to describe a beautiful man. To
her consternation, everything he said and did
intrigued her.

"Oddly enough you haven't changed since
last night," he remarked. "The concierge
said you resembled Aphrodite, a description
that fits you in every detail except for your
crutches."

She laughed to let him know she didn't
take him seriously. To believe him would be a
huge mistake. "Careful," she cautioned. "You
might just turn my head if you keep up that
malarkey."

One dark brow lifted. "Malarkey?"

"An English expression for nonsense."

His jet-black eyes came alive. "You mean my methods are working?" By now he'd devoured a roll and most of his salad.

"Absolutely. But since I won't be in Greece long, maybe your time would be better spent talking to someone of your own kind and background."

In an instant his jaw hardened. Uh-oh. She must have struck a nerve.

"*My own kind?*" The words came out more like a soft hiss.

She choked on her iced tea. What had she said to provoke such a reaction? "Surely you must realize I meant no offense. Perhaps the maid of honor wasn't to your liking last night, but I saw a lot of lovely Greek women at the reception—women who live here and would enjoy your attention."

Akis sat back in the chair. "Meaning you don't?"

"I didn't say that!" Their conversation had taken a strange twist.

"Let's start over again." He cocked his head. "We weren't formally introduced. My name is Akis Giannopoulos as you already know. What's yours?"

She took a deep breath. "Raina."

"Ah. Raina what?"

She shrugged her shoulders. "Does it matter when we'll never see each other again?"

"That's the second time you've used the same excuse not to tell me."

"I simply don't see the point." He grew on her with every moment they spent together. This wasn't supposed to happen!

An ominous silence surrounded them. "Obviously not. If you'll excuse me, I'm going to change clothes in the cabana."

She'd made him angry. Good. Raina wanted him to leave her alone. But as she watched him stride to the other side of the pool, she experienced a strange sense of loss totally at odds with her determination to separate herself from him.

Raina wanted to escape any more involvement because she had a premonition this man had the power to hurt her in a way not even Byron had done. Akis made her feel things she didn't want to feel. To give in to her desire to be with him could bring her joy, but for how long? When the excitement wore off for him, would he find someone else? Raina was afraid to trust what she was feeling. She quickly grabbed her crutches and hurried to find Chloe's mother who was in the kitchen.

"Thank you for the delicious lunch, Nora. Now if you don't mind, my ankle has started to ache again. I'm going to go to my room and lie down for a while. Please say goodbye to Mr. Giannopoulos for me. He came over to visit with you and is still out in the pool."

Her eyes widened. "Of course. Can I get you anything?"

"Not a thing. You've done too much for me already. I just need to rest my leg for a while."

"Then go on." The two women hugged and she left the kitchen for her suite of rooms. In truth Raina needed to get her mind off Akis. Since she hadn't had family around for a long time, it felt wonderful to be spoiled by two people who showed her so much love. Hopefully when Raina went back outside later, she'd find Akis gone.

With Chloe and Theo touring the fjords in Norway for the next two weeks, she hoped Akis wouldn't drop by until after the couple had returned from their honeymoon. After a few days' reunion in order to meet Theo, Raina would fly back to Monterey.

Akis took his time dressing. He knew instinctively Raina had said and done things to discourage him. Why? One of her stiletto-like jabs had worked its way under his skin and had taken hold.

How much did she know about him? Had she been insinuating that he wasn't good enough for her? Was it something Chloe had told her about his roots?

His own kind and background? Was he being paranoid?

Raina had rushed to explain what she'd meant when she'd told him he'd be better off spending time with his own kind and background instead of an American who'd be leaving soon. Even if he'd felt her sincerity and were willing to believe her explanation, the words had sunk deep in that vulnerable spot inside him and wouldn't go away.

He and Vasso were the brothers who'd climbed out of poverty without the benefit of formalized education. No college, no university degrees to hang on the wall. Akis wasn't well read or well traveled. He came out of that class of poor people who didn't have that kind of money, nor the sophistication. Whatever he and his brother had achieved had come through hard work.

No matter how much money he made now, it didn't give him the polish of someone like Theo who'd attended the finest university to become a banker like his father and grandfather before him. Akis could hold his own, but he was aware of certain inadequacies that would never change.

By now he got along fine in English, but being with her made him realize how much he didn't know about her language. He wasn't like Theo, who'd spent a year in England and spoke English with only a trace of accent.

Chloe could answer a lot of his questions, but she wasn't available and wouldn't be home for a fortnight. That presented a problem. Before long her former high school friend would be back in California. This woman worked in a lab? What kind? She could have meant anything.

His head was spinning with questions for which there were no answers. Not yet anyway.

When he left the cabana, he wasn't surprised

to find Raina had disappeared on him. She couldn't get away from him fast enough. On his way into the house he ran into Nora. Though tempted to ask questions he knew she could answer, he didn't want to drag her into something that was strictly between him and Raina.

"The wedding was beautiful. Now you can relax for a little while. Thank you for lunch."

"You're always welcome here. You know that. Raina's ankle was hurting and she went to her room. She asked me to say goodbye to you."

"I appreciate that. She did seem a little under the weather."

He kissed her cheek and left the house for the limo where his driver was waiting. "Take me to the office."

During the ride he sat back trying to figure out what was going on with her. She'd told his employee at the store her name was Ginger Moss, but the concierge denied any knowledge of it. Why in the hell had she done that?

Once back at the Giannopoulos business complex off Syntagma Square, he walked through the empty offices to his private suite. It was a good thing it was Sunday. In this mood he'd probably bite the heads off the staff.

Vasso would be back tomorrow, but Akis needed to talk to him. His brother was busy overseeing a new store opening in Heraklion. If not for the wedding, Akis would have gone with him.

He rang Vasso's cell phone number. It was four o'clock in the afternoon. He should still be at the grand opening to make sure everything went smoothly. "Pick up, Vasso." But it went through to his voice mail. Akis left the message for him to call ASAP. While he waited to hear from him, he caught up on some paperwork.

When his brother hadn't phoned him by seven-thirty, Akis couldn't take it anymore and decided to drive back to the Milonis estate. Before the night was out he would find out why she didn't want to let him into her life. Was it because she thought he was beneath her socially? Wasn't he good enough for her? If that was the case, then she needed to say that to his face.

Raina was different than any woman he'd ever met. He was deeply attracted not only to her looks but to her personality, as well. She could fight it all she wanted, but they had a connection. He just had to tear down that wall she'd put up. It was important to him.

Ione, the Milonises' housekeeper, met him at the door and explained that Chloe's parents had gone out for dinner, but they'd be back shortly.

"What about their houseguest?"

"Thespinis Maywood is in the den watching television."

Maywood...

So she hadn't run away quite yet. Pleased by the information he said, "I'll just say hello to her, then. Thanks, Ione." Without hesitation he walked past her and found his way to the room in question. Having been over here many times, he knew where to go.

The door was already open so he walked in to find her lying on the couch in front of the TV with a couple of throw pillows elevating her leg. She was dressed in the same jeans and T-shirt she'd worn earlier.

"That was quite a disappearing act you performed earlier," he stated from the doorway.

Her eyes met his calmly, as if she'd known he would show up again and was amused by it. Challenged by her deliberate pretense of indifference to him he said, "What does one call you? Ginger when you're with strangers, but just Raina with close friends?"

A sigh escaped her lips. After turning off the TV with the remote, she sat up and moved her legs to the floor. "I take it you went to the store where I fell." She stared hard at him. "I must admit I'm shocked that the clerk would give you my name. That's privileged information."

"Agreed, but it was false information. In case you were worried, I happen to own that store."

"What?" Those incredible lavender eyes of hers had suddenly turned a darker hue. At last something had shaken her out of her almost condescending attitude. Did she really not know how he earned his living? Because of her relationship with the Milonis family, he found it hard, if not impossible, to believe.

"I read the incident report written up in the back room. You gave my employee the name of Ginger Moss, age twenty-six. What name will I find if I ask you to show me your passport? It will be important when I pay your hospital bill. They'll need more information to correct the discrepancy on the record."

"My insurance will reimburse you." She rested her hands on the top of her thighs. "I sometimes go by the nickname Ginger."

"Because of your hair?"

Her eyes fell away. "Yes."

"Even if I were to believe you, that's neither here nor there. I want to know why you felt you had to maintain your lie with me when you're a close friend of the woman who married my best friend."

The silence deafened him.

"I'll find out the truth before long. Why not be honest with me now and get it over with?" he pressed.

"Is that the only reason you came over here again?"

"What do *you* think?"

More color filled her cheeks. "I—I wish I hadn't told you where I'd fallen."

"Since I found you here at Chloe's, it's a moot point."

She stirred restlessly. "You want me to apologize?"

Akis had her rattled, otherwise she wouldn't have asked those questions. He rubbed his lower lip with his thumb. "You want the truth from me? Do you think that's fair when you've exempted yourself from being forth-coming with me?"

She moistened her lips, drawing his attention to them. All night he'd wondered what she'd taste like. "I meant no harm."

"If that's the case, then why the deception?"

"Look—" She sounded exasperated. Her cheeks grew more flushed as she got to her feet and fitted the crutches beneath her arms. "I haven't had a meaningful relationship with a man for a long time because it's the way I've wanted it."

He walked over to her. "But clearly there've been a lot of men who've wanted one with you. You think I'm just another man you can ignore without telling me why?" She looked away quickly, letting him know he'd guessed the truth. "A woman with your looks naturally attracts a lot of unwanted attention. It must be galling to realize that whatever you did to put me off, fate had a hand in my showing up at Chloe's home. Prove to me my interest in you isn't wanted and I'll leave now."

She looked the slightest bit anxious. "Akis— I just don't think it wise to get to know you better."

"Why? Because you haven't been honest with me and there *is* a man back home you're involved with?"

"No," she volunteered so fast and emphatically, he believed her. "There's no one. This conversation is ridiculous."

"It would be if I didn't know that you're interested in me, too. But for some reason, you're afraid and are using the excuse of having to fly to California to put me off. I want to know why."

"I'm not afraid of you. That's absurd."

"Last night you cheated me out of a dance. I don't know about you, but I need to feel your mouth moving beneath mine or I might go a little mad with wanting."

"Please don't say things like that," she whispered.

"Because you know you want it, too?"

Her breathing sounded shallow. "Maybe I do, but I'm afraid."

"Of me?" He brushed his lips against hers.

"No. Not you. I'm afraid of my own feelings."

"Shall we find out if they're as strong as mine?" He wrapped her in his arms, crutches and all. His lips caught the small cry that escaped hers, giving him the opportunity to coax a deeper kiss from her. First one, then another, until she allowed him full access and the spark between them ignited into fire.

"Akis—" she cried softly before kissing him back with a hunger that thrilled him. He'd kissed other women, but nothing prepared him for the surge of desire driving both of them as they swayed together.

"I want you, Raina," he whispered against her creamy throat, "more than any woman I've ever wanted in my life." He came close to forgetting her sprained ankle until a moan sounded in her throat, prompting him to release her with reluctance and step away.

She steadied herself with the crutches for control. Those enticing lips looked swollen and thoroughly kissed. "That shouldn't have happened." The tremor in her voice was achingly real.

"But it did because we both wanted it." He took a quick breath. "I want to spend time with you, and from the way you kissed me, I know you want the same thing." His comment coincided with the arrival of Chloe's parents, who walked in on the two of them.

"Weren't you over here earlier?" Socus

teased him in his native tongue. "No wonder our guest didn't mind that we had an important business dinner to attend."

Akis shook his head. "She didn't know I was coming over again."

"We're glad you're here, Akis," Nora said in English. "We don't want her to leave. Please do what you can to persuade her to stay until Chloe and Theo get back."

Socus chimed in. "If we had our way, we'd insist on your living with us for a long time, young woman."

Raina's eyes misted over. "You're such dear people and have been wonderful to me. But I'm afraid I have too many responsibilities at home to remain here for any length of time."

"Your ankle needs at least a week to heal before we let you get on a plane," Chloe's father declared. "But we can talk more about this in the morning. Good night, you two."

After they left the room Akis said, "Your ankle could use more rest. There's nothing I'd like better than to help you pass the time."

He sensed she knew she was defeated, but that didn't stop her from darting him a piercing glance. "What about your work?"

"My brother will fill in for me. We do it for

each other when necessary." He stood there with his hands on his hips. "You look tired, so I'm going to leave. If I come over in the morning, will I still find you here?"

Her eyes flashed. "Perhaps the question should be, will you show up since you have a disparaging opinion of me?"

"You mean after you told me I should stick with my own kind and background?"

She stirred restlessly. "I can see you still haven't forgiven me for an innocent remark."

"There was nothing innocent about it. But the way you kissed me back a few minutes ago confirms my original gut instinct that you know something significant has happened to both of us. Good night, *thespinis*."

He left the house for the limo. On the way to his penthouse his cell phone rang. One look at the caller ID and he clicked on. "Vasso? How come it's taken you so long to get back to me?"

"Nice talking to you, too, bro."

His head reared. "Sorry."

"The phone died on me and I just got back to my hotel to recharge it. What's wrong? You don't sound like yourself."

"That's because I'm not."

"The opening went fine."

Akis was in such a state he'd forgotten to ask. "Sorry. My mind is on something else."

"Was there a problem at the wedding? I saw you on the evening news helping a beautiful woman on crutches into the limo."

So Vasso saw it. "She's the reason I called. When will you be back?"

His brother laughed. "I'll fly in around 7:00 a.m. and should be at the office by nine."

"If you're that late, I'm afraid I won't be there."

"That sounded cryptic. Why?"

"Something happened at the reception."

"You sound odd. What is it?"

"I've…met someone."

"I'm not even going to try to figure that one out. Just tell me what has you so damned upset."

"Believe it or not, a woman has come into my life."

"There've been several women in your life over the years. Tell me something I don't know. Are we talking about the woman on crutches?"

"Yes. This one is different." Both brothers had led a bachelor life for so long, not even Akis believed what had happened to him since he'd seen Raina on the street.

"Are you saying what I think you're saying?"

"Yes."

"You're serious."

"Yes."

Vasso exhaled sharply. "She feels the same way?"

His teeth snapped together. "After the way she kissed me back tonight, I'd stake my life on it."

"But you only met her last evening."

"I know. She looks like Aphrodite with lavender eyes."

"I'll admit she was a stunner." Laughter burst out of Vasso. "But you sound like you still need to sleep off the champagne."

"I swear I only had a sip."

"Come on, Akis. Quit the teasing."

"I'm not." For the first time in his life Akis was swimming in uncharted waters where a woman was concerned.

A long silence ensued. "How old is she?"

"Twenty-six."

"From Athens?"

"No. California."

"She's an American?"

"Yes. On the day of the wedding rehearsal, we almost bumped into each other on the sidewalk after I left Theo at the bank. I couldn't get her out of my head. On the night of the reception, to my surprise she was sitting at a table in the back of the ballroom.

"When I asked her to dance, she didn't understand because she said she didn't speak Greek. But she couldn't dance anyway because she was on crutches. I helped her out to the limo and took her to her hotel."

"Just like that you spent the night with her? You've never done anything like that before. Wasn't that awfully fast?"

"I didn't stay with her and you don't know all that happened. When I couldn't find her at the hotel today and learned she'd checked out, I checked with Theo's family. They hadn't heard of her so I decided to go over to Chloe's for help. When I went walked in, to my shock I found her relaxing at the side of the pool."

"She was at Chloe's?"

"Yes. It seems Chloe spent a school year with her back in high school on one of those exchange programs to learn English."

"How come you've never heard of her?"

"I once remember Theo telling me that Chloe had an American friend she lived with in high school, but I never made the connection."

"What's her name?"

"Raina Maywood. But when she fell and sprained her ankle in our number four store, she gave Galen a different name before going to the ER. I had a devil of a time tracking her down."

"Wait, wait—start over again. You're not making sense."

"Nothing has made sense since we first saw each other."

"Akis? Are you still with me?"

"Yes."

"What's your gut telling you?"

"I don't know," he confessed.

"Maybe she wanted to meet you. It wouldn't be hard to connect the dots. After all, she knows the circles Chloe's family runs in. Maybe when Chloe invited her to come to the wedding, she told her about Theo's best man and promised to introduce you."

"There's a flaw in that thinking, Vasso, because it didn't happen that way. By sheer chance I asked her to dance. Otherwise we would never have met. After I took her to her hotel, she made it close to impossible for me to find her."

"But she *did* end up at Chloe's, so it's my guess she hoped you'd show up there at some point. Even if that part of the evening wasn't planned, what if all along her agenda has been to come to the wedding and use Chloe's parents to meet you? Is that what you're afraid of? That she's after your money?"

"Hell if I know."

"It stands to reason Chloe would have told her all about Theo's best man. There's no sin in it, but the way things are moving so fast, don't you think you need to take a step back until more time passes? Then you can see what's real and what isn't. Think about it."

Akis *was* thinking. His big brother had touched on one of Akis's deepest fears. The possibility that somehow she'd engineered their meeting like other women in the past had done tore him up inside. He wanted to believe that everything about their meeting and the unfolding of events had been entirely spontaneous.

But if Chloe had discussed him with Raina, then her comment about his background made a lot of sense. He and Vasso were the brothers who'd climbed out of poverty to make their way in the world. They lacked the essentials that other well-bred people took for granted— like monetary help from family, school scholarships, exposure to the world.

They'd been marked from birth as the brothers who'd come out of that class of poor people who would be lucky to survive. Whatever he and Vasso had achieved had come through sheer hard work.

Akis could hold his own, but he was aware of certain inadequacies that would never change.

If in the past the situation had warranted it, he and Vasso had always given each other good advice. But this one time he didn't want to hear it even though he was the one who'd called his brother.

Akis didn't want to think Raina might be like Althea who was looking for a husband who could keep her in the style of Chloe's parents.

"Isn't that why you phoned me, because you're worried?" his brother prodded. "She's seen the kind of wealth Chloe comes from. You remember how crazy Sofia and I were over each other when we lived on the island without a drachma to our name?"

"How could I forget?"

"But she turned down my wedding proposal because she said she could do better. It wasn't until our business started to flourish that she started chasing me again and wouldn't leave me alone. At that point I wasn't interested in her anymore."

"I remember everything," Akis's voice grated. Both he and Vasso had been through the painful experience of being used. It had made them wary of stronger attachments. A few years ago when they'd set up two charities to honor their parents, one of the women they'd hired as a secretary to deal with the paperwork had made a play for Vasso. But it turned out she wanted marriage rather than the job.

Akis had run into a similar situation with an attractive woman they'd hired to run one of their stores. She'd called Akis one evening claiming there was an emergency. When he showed up at the store, it turned out the emergency was a ploy to get him alone.

Most women they met were introduced to them by mutual friends. After a few dates it was clear they had marriage and money on their minds. But the essential bonding of two minds and hearts of the kind he saw in Theo and Chloe's relationship always seemed to be missing.

"Sorry to be such a downer, but Chloe's friend did lie about her name, which I find strange. When are you going to see her again?"

"I told her I'd be over tomorrow."

"Did she tell you *not* to come?"

He grimaced. "No." But earlier she'd told him he'd be better off to find a woman of his own kind and background because she was leaving Greece. She'd been keeping up that mantra to hide what was really wrong.

"Okay. As I see it, maybe she's taking advantage of her friendship with Chloe. Then again, maybe there is no agenda here. All I can say is, slow down."

Akis took a deep breath, more confused than ever over her mixed signals. Why would she have flown all the way to Greece, yet she hadn't attended the wedding of her good friend at the church? Bombarded by a series of conflicting emotions, he felt a negative burst of adrenaline, not knowing what to believe.

"I don't want to think about it anymore tonight. Thanks for listening. I'll see you in the morning." He clicked off.

Without that kiss he might have decided it wasn't worth it to pursue her further, except that he didn't really believe that. It had taken all his willpower not to chase around the corner after her with some excuse to detain her. But this evening he hadn't been thinking clearly. The need to feel her in his arms outweighed every other thought. *It still did...*

"Kyrie?" his driver called to him. "We've arrived."

So they had. Akis thanked him and climbed out of the limo. On his way up to the penthouse, he went over the conversation with his brother. Vasso had given him one piece of advice he would follow from here on out.

Slow down.

CHAPTER THREE

BY THE TIME Raina had unwrapped her ankle to shower on Monday morning, she had to admit it felt a lot better. Resting it had really helped because there was little swelling now. It didn't need to be rewrapped as long as she walked with crutches and was careful.

After dressing in a blouse and jeans, she brushed her hair and put on her pink lipstick. Every time she thought about Akis Giannopoulos, she got a fluttery feeling in her chest, the kind there was no remedy for.

Her lips still throbbed from the passion his mouth had aroused. For a little while she'd been swept away to a place she'd never been before. After having no personal life for so long, she supposed something like this had been inevitable. Maybe it was good this hormone rush had happened here in Greece. Before long she'd be leaving, so whatever it was she felt for this man, their relationship would be short-lived.

Since she couldn't do any sightseeing this trip, her only option was to stay at Chloe's. Such inactivity for a man like Akis would wear thin. When he found himself bored, he'd find a plausible reason to leave.

Breakfast came and went. She lounged by the pool and read a book she'd brought. Every time Nora or a maid came out to see if she wanted anything, she expected Akis to follow. By lunchtime she decided he wasn't coming.

After kissing her as payback for the way she'd treated him last night, he'd left the house. It wouldn't surprise her if he'd had no intention of coming back today. Raina ought to be relieved. Once she'd eaten lunch with Nora, there was still no sign of him.

Hating to admit to herself she was disappointed he hadn't come, she went to her bedroom to do some business on the phone with her staff running the estate in California. No sooner had she gotten off the phone than the maid knocked on her door. "Kyrie Giannopoulos is waiting for you on the patio."

At the news her heart jumped, a terrible

sign that he mattered to her much more than she wanted him to. "I'll be right there." She refreshed her lipstick before using her crutches to make it out to the pool area where Akis was waiting for her.

His intense black gaze swept over her while he stood beneath the awning in an open-necked tan sport shirt and jeans. His clothes covered a well-defined chest and rock-hard legs. Whether he wore a tux, a bathing suit or casual clothes, her legs turned to mush just looking at him.

"I would have been here sooner, but my business meeting this morning took longer than I'd supposed. The housekeeper told me you've already had lunch. Have you ever been to Athens?"

"I came here once with my grandparents when I was young, but remember very little."

"What happened to your parents?"

"They were killed in a light plane crash when I was twelve."

"How awful for you."

"I could hardly believe it when it happened. I suffered for years. We had such a wonderful life together. They were my best friends."

"I'm sorry," he whispered.

"So am I, but I was very blessed to have marvelous grandparents who did everything for me."

"Thank heaven for that." He eyed her thoughtfully. "Are you up to some sightseeing then?"

Her breath caught. "Much as I'd love to tour Athens, I can't. You didn't need to come over. A phone call would have sufficed."

"You can see Athens from my penthouse terrace." She blinked. "The city will be at your feet. I have a powerful telescope that will enable you to see its famous sights up close from the comfort of a chair and ottoman for your leg."

"Go with him, Raina," Chloe's mother urged, having just walked out on the patio. "Socus and I went up there one night. You can see everything in the most wonderful detail. The Acropolis at twilight is like a miracle."

Raina couldn't very well turn him down with an endorsement like that from Nora. "You've sold me. I'll just go back to the room for my purse." Reaching for her crutches, she hurried away with a pounding heart. Retrieving her purse, she headed for the front door, but Akis was there first to open it for her.

"Thank you," she whispered, so aware of his presence it was hard to think. Once he'd helped her inside the limo out in front, he sat across from her. "I know you want to rest your leg so I've told the driver to take us straight to the Giannopoulos complex."

"We could have stayed at Chloe's and played cards. It would have saved you all this trouble."

The compelling male mouth that had kissed her so thoroughly last night broke into a smile, turning her heart over. "Some trouble is worth it."

She looked out the window without seeing anything. Going to his penthouse wasn't a good idea, but her hectic emotions had taken over her common sense. Raina wanted to be with him. She would only stay awhile before she asked him to take her back to Chloe's.

The driver turned into a private alley and stopped at the rear of the office building. Akis helped her out and drew a remote from his pocket that opened a door to a private elevator. In less than a minute they'd shot to the roof and the door opened again.

Adjusting her crutches, Raina followed him into his glassed in, air-conditioned penthouse. No woman's touch here, no curtains, no frills or knickknacks. Only chrome and earth tones. It was a man's domicile through and through, yet she saw nothing of his dynamic personality reflected.

The best man who'd tracked her down despite all odds didn't seem to fit in these unimaginative surroundings. But she could understand his coming home to this at night. Glorious Athens lay below them from every angle.

"Come out to the terrace. I have everything set up for you."

The telescope beckoned beneath the overhang. Working her crutches, she stepped out in the warm air and flashed him a glance. "Were you an eagle in another life? I like your eyrie very much."

"As far as I know, this is the only life I've been born to, but I was hatched in a very different place as you well know."

She frowned. No, she didn't know. Akis was trying to rile her. In retaliation she refused to rise to the bait.

He took her crutches so she could sit on the leather chair and prop her leg on the ottoman. After putting the crutches aside, he placed the telescope so she could look through it while she sat there. "I've set it on the Acropolis and the Parthenon."

"The cradle of Western civilization," she murmured. "This is the perfect spot to begin my tour. Thank you." One look and she couldn't believe it. "Oh, Akis—I feel like I'm right there. How fabulous! A picture doesn't do it justice. Do you mind if I move this around a little? There's so much to see, I could look through it for hours."

"That's why I brought you here. Enjoy any view you want. Since it's heating up outside, I'll get us some lemonade."

She was glad he'd left. The brief intimacy they'd shared last night hadn't lasted long enough. The fire between them had been building since he'd shown up at Chloe's house. But he was only gone for a few minutes and returned with a drink for both of them. The second he came back out, her pulse raced.

He lounged against the edge of a wrought-iron patio table and played tour director for the next two hours. Akis was a fount of information, responding to all her questions.

No one watching them would know how

disturbed she was to be this close to such a man who on the surface appeared so pleasant. Underneath his urbane facade Raina knew he was just biding his time until she tired of sightseeing and he had her full attention.

When she'd eventually run out of questions, she sat back with a sigh. "Thanks to you, I feel like I've walked all over this city without missing anything important. I'll remember your kindness when I watch the city recede from my plane window."

Akis moved the telescope out of reach, then flicked her a probing glance. "Forget about returning to California. You've only seen a portion of Athens. What you haven't seen is what I consider to be the best part of Greece. I'm prepared to show it to you. I understand Chloe's parents have extended you an open invitation to stay for a while."

She shook her head. "Why would you want to do anything for me when it's obvious you have issues with me?"

"Maybe because you're different from the other women I've met and I'm intrigued."

"That's not the answer and you know it."

One black brow lifted. "You can't deny the chemistry between us. I'm still breathless from the explosion when we got in each other's arms last night."

Raina's hands gripped the arms of the chair. "So am I."

"After such honesty, you still want to run from me?" he said in a husky tone.

"Physical attraction gets in the way of common sense."

He folded his arms. "What is your common sense telling you?"

"I think your questions about me have fueled your interest."

"Is that wrong?"

"Not wrong, just unsettling. I know you've been upset with me since the night of the reception when I wouldn't tell you my name and gave your employee a different name. I already told you the reason why."

"Just not all of it," he challenged in that maddening way, causing her blood pressure to soar.

"What's the matter with you?" she cried softly. "Earlier today you accused me of knowing something about your origins, when in truth I know next to nothing about you except that you were the best man!" Her voice shook with emotion. "If there's some sinister secret you're anxious to hide, I promise you I don't know what it is."

His eyes narrowed on her features. "That's difficult for me to believe when you've been Chloe's best friend for years."

She nodded. "We became best friends and have seen and stayed in touch with each other over the years. I knew she was crazy about Theo months ago, but I only heard she was getting married a month ago. She was so full of excitement over the wedding plans, I didn't even know the last name of her fiancé's best man, let alone any details about you. If that offends your male pride, I'm sorry."

He shifted his weight. "I'm afraid it's you *I've* offended without realizing it. Shall we call a truce and start over? Nora wants us to come back and eat dinner with them by the pool. Afterward they're going to show us the wedding video."

"You can tell they're missing Chloe," she said.

"That's what happens when there's an only child."

Raina knew all about that and agreed with him. "Their family is very close. Just being with them this little bit makes me surprised they allowed her to leave home for the school year."

"If she hadn't been happy with you, I'm sure she wouldn't have stayed." While she felt his deep voice resonate, his gaze traveled over her. "Surely you can understand how much they want to pay you back for the way your family made her feel so welcome. If you want my opinion, I think you'll hurt their feelings if you fly to the States too soon, but it's your call."

Privately Raina feared the same thing. "I'm sure you're right. If I stay until Chloe and Theo get back, it'll give me a chance to rest my leg a little more." *More days to spend with Akis.*

Wasn't that the underlying factor in her decision just now, even though her heart was warning her to run from him as fast as she could? To love this man meant opening herself up to pain from which she might never recover.

"They'll be happy to hear it. Are you ready to go back?"

No, her heart cried, but her lips said "Yes."

After she finished her drink, he helped her with the crutches. Their hands brushed, sending darts of sensation running up her arms. He didn't try to take advantage, but it didn't matter. Every look or touch from him sensitized her body. As they left the penthouse for the drive back to the Milonis estate, she fought to ignore her awareness of him.

Later, after a delicious dinner, Akis took the crutches from Raina while she settled on the couch in the den. Nora sat next to her while Socus started the video. Akis turned off the light and sat in one of the upholstered chairs to watch. Cries of excitement, happiness and laughter from Chloe's parents punctuated the scene of the wedding day unfolding before their eyes.

The videographer had captured everything from the moment Chloe left the house for the church. Parts of the ceremony in the church left Raina in happy tears for her dear friend. She just knew they'd have a wonderful life together.

Other parts of the film covered the reception, including the dancing. The camera panned from the wedding couple to the best man dancing with the maid of honor. "You and Althea make a beautiful couple," Socus exclaimed.

Raina concurred. He was so handsome it hurt, but the inscrutable expression on his face was distinctly different from the adoring look on Althea's. Suddenly the camera focused on the guests. Raina saw herself at the table. Shock!

But there were more shocks when it caught Akis accompanying her from the ballroom. She'd had no idea they were being filmed.

Nora laughed. "Oh, Akis… Now I understand why you didn't spend the rest of the evening with poor Althea. You remind me of the prince at the ball who avoided the stepsisters because he wanted to know the name of the mystery woman on crutches and ended up running after her." Socus's laughter followed.

In that instant Raina's gaze fused with a pair of jet black eyes glinting in satisfaction over Nora's observation. Her body broke out in guilty heat.

"Wasn't I lucky that I found Cinderella at your house."

"We're very happy you did." Nora beamed.

"It saved me from prowling the countryside for the maiden with the crutches."

Chloe's mother chuckled. "Wait till Chloe and Theo watch this. They're going to love it."

"They will," Raina agreed with her before lowering her blond head. Chloe would appreciate the irony of the camera finding her friend from California in the crowd despite every effort Raina had made to stay away from the camcorders of the paparazzi.

While she sat there wishing she could escape to her bedroom, Akis got to his feet and turned on the light. "Thank you for dinner and an entertaining evening. Now I know Raina needs to rest her leg, so I'm going to leave."

"So soon?" Nora questioned.

"I'm afraid so. But I'll be by in the morning at nine. Earlier I told Raina I'd like to show her another part of Greece I know she'll enjoy while she's still recovering." His dark eyes probed hers. "But maybe you've decided you'd rather stay here."

He'd deliberately put her on the spot. Everyone was waiting for her answer. Not wanting to seem ungracious she said, "No. I'll be ready. Thank you."

"Good."

The pilot landed the helicopter on the pad of the Milonis estate. Akis could see Raina's gleaming blond hair as she stood on her crutches. It wasn't until you got closer that you noticed that hint of red in the strands. His gaze fell over her curvaceous figure that did wonders for the summery denims and short-sleeved small-print blouse she was wearing.

He opened the doors of the Giannopoulos company's recently purchased five-seater copter. "Let me take your crutches and handbag." Once she'd handed them to him, he put them aside, then picked up her gorgeous body by the waist. The instant there was contact, her warmth and fragrance enveloped him.

Without letting go of her, he helped her into the seat next to the window behind the pilot. That way he could keep an eye on her from the copilot's seat. "Are you all right?" Their mouths were only inches apart.

"Y-yes," came her unsteady voice before she looked away. A nerve jumped madly at the base of her creamy throat. The touch of skin against skin had affected her, too.

"Have you ever flown in a helicopter before?"

She nodded.

After laying the crutches on the floor, he

put her purse in the storage unit, and then looked down at her.

"Are you all strapped in?"

"Yes. I'm fine. I just want to know where we're going."

"Are you afraid I'm planning to carry you off, never to be seen again?"

A secret smile appeared. "After the fierce look on your face as you headed toward my table at the hotel, the thought did occur to me."

Charmed despite his questions about what she was still hiding from him he said, "I'll give you a clue. We're headed for the Ionian Sea. Once we reach the water, I'll give you a blow-by-blow account using the microphone. But there's one more thing I have to do before takeoff."

Akis pulled out several pillows from a locker and hunkered down to elevate her leg. She wore sandals. His hands slid beneath her calf and heel to adjust the fit. He ran a finger over her ankle, pleased to notice she trembled. "There's no trace of swelling I can see," he said, eyeing her. "We'll make sure things stay that way today."

The urge to kiss her was overwhelming,

but he restrained himself. Her thank-you followed him to his seat. He gave the pilot a nod, put on his sunglasses and strapped himself in. Before long Athens receded and they were arcing their way in a northwesterly direction. Over the mic he gave her a geography lesson and responded to her questions.

When they reached the island of Corfu surrounded by brilliant blue water, he had the pilot swing lower so she could take in the fascinating sight of whitewashed houses. Here and there he pointed out a Byzantine church and the remains of several Venetian fortresses.

He shot Raina a speaking glance. "I brought you here first. This is where Poseidon fell in love with Korkyra, the Naiad nymph."

"Ah. Poseidon…" Her lips curved upward. "Did Korkyra reciprocate his feelings?"

"According to legend she adored him and they had a baby named Phaiax. Today the islanders have the nickname Phaeacians. Another island in this group is fourteen miles south of here. We'll head there now."

"What is it called?"

"Paxos. When you see it, you'll understand why it's constantly photographed."

In a few minutes he heard a cry. "What a darling island!" That wasn't the word he would have chosen, but he was pleased by her response. "What kind of vegetation is that?"

"Olive groves. Some of the gnarled trees are ancient. The pilot will fly us over the western side and you'll see steep, chalky white cliffs. If you look closely, you'll spot its many caves along the coast line. When you go into them on a launch, they glow blue."

"How beautiful!"

"We have Poseidon to thank for its creation. He wanted to get away from stress on the big island of Corfu, so he used his trident to create this hideaway for him and his wife."

"Or maybe to hide his wife from Korkyra? What are you saying? That the stress of having a mistress and keeping his wife happy at the same time was too much, even for a god?" Like a discordant note, he heard brittle laughter come out of her. "That's hilarious!"

There was a story behind her hollow reaction, but now was not the time to explore it. "The Greek myths are meant to be entertaining. If you'll notice, there's another tinier island just beyond this one called Anti Paxos. When Poseidon wanted to be strictly alone, he came here to swim in the clear green water you can see below."

"I imagine that leading a double life would have worn him out."

Laughter burst from Akis.

"Wasn't *he* lucky to be a god and pick the most divine area in his immortal world to plan his next conquest." The pilot circled Anti Paxos for a closer look. "What a heavenly spot."

It was. Akis's favorite place on earth. He wanted to hide Raina away here, away from the world where the two of them could be together and make love for the rest of time.

Unfortunately they'd come to the end of the tour. He checked his watch. "We're going to head back to Athens via a little different route. We'll be crossing over a portion of Albania you should find fascinating. If you're thirsty or hungry, there's bottled water and snacks in the seat pouch in front of you."

"Um. Don't mind if I do. Would you or the pilot like something?"

That was thoughtful of her. "We're fine."

In a minute she said, "These almonds are the best I've ever tasted!"

"They're grown on these islands." Akis was addicted to them.

"How would it be to live right down there in paradise! If I did, I'm sure I'd become an addict."

Everything she said and did entrenched her deeper in his heart. She had a sweetness and vulnerability that made him want to protect her. Raina had become his addiction and already he couldn't imagine life without her. That's when he realized he was in serious trouble, but for once in his life he didn't care.

"If you'll extend your time in Greece, I can arrange for you to stay on Anti Paxos. Think about it and let me know after we get back to Chloe's house."

"Even if I could take time off from work, what about yours? Can you afford to be gone any longer?"

His heart leaped. So she *was* interested…

"My brother will cover for me."

"You're lucky to have him." She sounded sincere. "Is there more family?"

"No. Just Vasso."

"Is he younger? Older?"

The questions were coming at last. "Older by eleven months."

"You were almost twins!"

"Almost."

"Do you resemble each other?"

He turned to his pilot. "What do you think?" he asked in Greek. "Do Vasso and I look alike?"

The other man grinned before giving him an answer.

Akis translated. "He said, superficially."

"Is Vasso married?"

Why did she want to know that? "Not yet."

"Then maybe you should arrange for him to meet Chloe's bridesmaid."

His black brows furrowed. "I'm afraid my brother prefers to be the one in pursuit. What makes you so concerned for Althea?"

"Even Nora noticed how crestfallen she looked when you stopped dancing with her."

"According to Theo, she has lots of boyfriends."

"But she wanted *you*," Raina came back.

"Why do you say that?"

"I may have been farther away, but I could see her disappointment. Think how much she would have enjoyed a day like this with you."

"If you're trying to make me feel guilty, it isn't working."

She flashed him a quick smile. "Not at all. I was just thinking how fortunate I've been to be given a fantastic personal tour narrated by you. It's a real thrill."

"I'm glad you're enjoying it. But it's not over yet. We'll be flying over a portion of the Pindus National Park covered in black pines. The view from this altitude is extraordinary." While she studied the landscape, he'd feast his eyes on her.

For the next hour she appeared captivated by the unfolding scenery. Every now and again he heard a little gasp of awe as they dipped lower to view a new sight. Whatever his suspicions might have been in the beginning, her barrage of questions made him think her reactions to the beauty below them couldn't be faked.

Once they'd landed on the pad of the Milonis estate, he helped Raina down. Their bodies brushed, causing a tiny gasp to escape her lips. He knew exactly how she felt and didn't know how long he could stand it before he kissed her again.

Akis watched her disappear before he used the guest bathroom and phoned his driver to come to the house. He had plans for him and Raina later. After washing his hands, he walked out to the patio to phone his brother. No doubt he was still at the office. Akis needed to give him a heads-up that he wouldn't be coming in to work for a few days. He was taking a brief vacation in order to spend time with Raina.

To his frustration, his call went to Vasso's voice mail. Once again he had to ask him to call him back ASAP. Then he spoke to his private secretary to know if there were any situations he needed to hear about. But he was assured everything was fine. Vasso had been there until two o'clock, then he'd left.

After hanging up, he walked to the cabana and changed into a swimming suit. Akis needed a workout after sitting so long. Much as he wanted Raina to join him in the pool, he knew she couldn't. But on that score he was wrong. When he'd finished his laps and started to get out, he saw her at the shallow end, floating on her back. The crutches had been left at the side of the pool.

By rotating her arms, she was able to move around without hurting her ankle. He swam over to her, noticing her blond hair looked darker now that it was wet and swept back.

The classic features of her oval face revealed her pure beauty. Those eyes shimmered like amethysts. *Incredible.*

"I'm glad you came out here."

"After today's tour, I thought I'd like to see what it was like to swim with Poseidon, god of the sea."

He sucked in his breath. "You're not afraid I might make you my next conquest?"

She kept on moving. "Do you think you can?"

He kept up with her. "After our kiss the other night, I think you know the answer to that."

"What will your wife say?"

"She doesn't rule my life."

"That would be the worst fate for you, wouldn't it? To be ruled by your passion for one woman? To be her slave forever?"

"Not if she's the right woman."

"How will you know when you've found her?" The pulse throbbing violently in the vulnerable spot of her throat betrayed her.

"I think I have. Stay in Greece until I can unveil all of the real you."

"The real me?"

"Yes. There's more to you than you want to let on."

A beguiling smile broke the corners of her mouth. "And what about you, swimming into my life? Who are you, really?"

He swam closer. "Who would you like me to be?" The blood pounded in his ears.

"Just yourself."

Raina...

She'd reached for the side of the pool and clung to it. "Akis," she said softly. "I'm frightened because my feelings for you are already too strong."

"Strong enough to meet me halfway and kiss me again?"

"I want to." Her voice throbbed. "But I'm worried I'll be enslaved by you."

Akis took a deep breath and moved through the water next to her. "Don't you know you're the one who has enslaved me? I need you, Raina."

Her eyes looked glazed. "You're not the only one," she confessed.

He clasped her to him and covered her trembling mouth with his own. This time he'd jumped right into the fire, heedless of the flames licking through his body.

Her curves melted against him as if she were made for him. He kissed her with growing abandon until he felt her hungry response. It wasn't like anything he'd ever known and he was afraid he'd never get enough.

"Raina," he whispered in a thick tone. "Do you have any idea how beautiful you are? How much I want you?"

She moaned her answer, too swallowed up in their need for each other to talk. This was what Akis had been waiting for all his life, this feeling of oneness and ecstasy.

"Anyone for dinner?" came the sudden godlike voice of thunder.

Raina made a sound in her throat and tore her lips from his. "Socus has seen us."

"He has to know what's going on," Akis whispered against the side of her neck. "You're a grown woman."

"Yes, but I'm also a guest in their home. What must he think when we only met a few days ago?"

"That we're incredibly lucky and are enjoying ourselves."

She lifted anxious eyes to him. "Way too much." To his regret she eased away from him in her orange bikini to reach the steps of the pool. After grabbing her towel and crutches, she disappeared inside the house.

Akis threw his dark head back and drank in gulps of air. No doubt Chloe's father had seen the two of them locked together while the water sizzled around them.

Naturally Raina would bring out a protective instinct in the older man. She was their honored guest. Akis swam to the deep end. After levering himself over the edge, he headed for the cabana to shower and get dressed.

As he was pulling on his crew neck, his cell rang. He drew it from his pant pocket to look at the caller ID and clicked on. "Vasso? Did you get my message?"

"Yes, but we've got an electrical problem at the number ten store I've got to see about. I'm leaving the penthouse to take care of it now. Before you go away on vacation, I've left some papers for you to look at in the den."

"About that new property we were thinking about on Crete?"

"No. It's something else. Talk to you later." He hung up before Akis could question him further.

Something else? What exactly did that

mean? Curious over it, Akis left the cabana in a slightly different mood than before and walked around the pool to the covered portion of the patio. Everyone was seated at the table waiting for him. Raina looked a golden vision wearing a pale yellow beach robe over her beautiful body.

"Ah, there you are," Nora exclaimed. "Now we can eat."

"I'm sorry to keep you waiting. My brother called me about a business problem. After dinner, I'll have to get back to the penthouse to deal with it." His gaze darted to Raina whose eyes were asking questions not even he could answer yet. "I'll phone you later about our plans for tomorrow." The night he'd planned with her would have to wait.

Raina watched Akis's tall, powerful body disappear from the patio in a few swift strides. Disappointment swept over her. She despised her weakness for remaining silent when he announced in front of Chloe's parents he'd call her later about plans for the next day. To them the silence on her part meant agreement and she'd be staying in Greece longer.

After the two of them had come close to

kissing each other senseless out in the pool, he would naturally assume she couldn't wait to be with him again. Socus had seen them kissing and had been left in no doubt what was going on between them.

That kiss had been her fault for taunting Akis. In some part of her psyche she'd wanted him to pull her into his arms. Otherwise she wouldn't have gotten into the pool. She knew she'd come to the edge of a cliff like the kind they'd flown over earlier in the day. One more false step and she'd fall so deep and hard for this man, she'd never recover. Raina couldn't forget a certain conversation with him.

What will your wife say?

She doesn't rule my life.

That would be the worst fate for you, wouldn't it? To be ruled by your passion for one woman? To be her slave forever?

Not if she's the right woman.

Raina didn't believe there was a right woman for a man as exciting and virile as Akis. In time he would tire of his latest lover and be caught by another woman who appealed to him. In an instant he'd go in pursuit.

The bitter taste of Byron's betrayal still lingered. It was time to end this madness with

Akis. But she'd promised Chloe's parents she'd wait to leave Greece until after Chloe and Theo got home from their honeymoon.

Once dinner was over, she went to her room. Though it was early, she took a shower and got ready for bed. She knew Akis would phone her.

If you know what's good for you, don't get in any deeper with him, Raina.

CHAPTER FOUR

AKIS LET HIMSELF in the penthouse and walked back to the den. He saw some papers placed on the table next to the computer. They looked like printouts. His brother had handwritten him a note he'd left on top of the keyboard. Akis sat down in the swivel chair and started to read.

Don't get mad at me for what I've done. You're so damn honorable, I knew you'd let your questions about Raina Maywood eat you alive. So I decided to put you out of your misery and play PI so she can't accuse you of stalking her. For what it's worth, you're going to bless me for what I've done.

Start with the printout of the article from a California newspaper, then work through the rest. Any worry you've been carrying around about her intentions has flown out the window. There's so much stuff about her, it'll blow your mind.

When you told me her last name was Maywood and that she was a friend of Chloe's from California, it got me thinking about the two helicopters we purchased. No wonder Chloe's parents allowed her to stay with Raina, the granddaughter of a man who was one of the pillars of the American economy.

Dazed at this point, Akis picked up the top sheet dated nine months ago.

An American icon of aerospace technology is dead at ninety-two. Joseph Maywood died at his estate in Carmel-by-the-Sea after a long bout of stomach cancer. At his side was his beautiful granddaughter, Laraine Maywood, twenty-six, now heiress to the massive multibillion-dollar Maywood fortune. His wife, Ginger Moss, daughter of famous California seascape artist Edwin Moss, passed away from heart failure several years earlier.

Kaching, kaching, kaching.

Pieces of the puzzle were falling into place faster than Akis could absorb them. Nonplussed, he sat staring at the ceiling. She was an *heiress*…

Adrenaline gushed through his veins.

The X Jet Explorer, built by Pacificopter Inc., was a company owned by the Maywood Corporation in California, USA. Suddenly pure revelation flowed through him. Akis jumped to his feet, incredulous. She was *that* Maywood.

Absolutely stunned, he reached for the next printout dated four years back.

Scandal rocks world-renowned Carmel-by-the Sea, a European-style California village nestled above a picturesque white-sand beach and home to beautiful heiress-apparent Laraine Maywood Wallace of the Maywood Corporation.

Wallace? He swallowed hard. She'd been married.

He looked back at the paper and kept reading.

Reputed to be a lookalike for the famous French actress and beauty Cath-

erine Deneuve in her youth, she has divorced husband Byron Wallace, the writer and biographer involved in a sensational, messy affair with Hollywood would-be starlet Isabel Granger who was also involved with her director boyfriend.

Akis groaned.

Only now could he understand Raina's brittle laughter during an earlier conversation. *What are you saying? That the stress of having a mistress and keeping his wife happy at the same time was too much, even for a god?* He could feel his gut twisting.

Vasso had left a postscript on his note.

You've got a green light, bro. No more worry. She's interested in you, not your money.

He scanned the other sheets, astonished over the two charities she'd started in California in honor of her grandparents, including all she'd accomplished as CEO of the Maywood megacorporation.

These revelations had turned him inside

out. It shamed him that he'd been so hard on her in his own mind when she'd suffered such pain in her life. The loss of her parents and grandparents…the betrayal by a man who had never deserved her…

"I hoped I'd find you here. How come you don't seem happier?"

Akis had been so absorbed and troubled, he hadn't heard his brother enter the den. He turned in his direction. "I didn't think you'd be back this soon."

"There was a power-grid failure, but it was soon repaired. I'm going to ask you again. What's wrong?"

He rubbed the back of his neck. "I feel like I've trespassed over her soul."

Vasso shook his head. "What are you talking about?"

"This information changes everything." It had been a humbling lesson that had left him shaken.

"Of course it does, but your reaction doesn't make sense."

"I can't explain right now." He squeezed Vasso's shoulder. "You're the best. I'll get back to you."

He left the printouts on the desk and hurried out of the penthouse, calling for his limo. Before he left for Chloe's house, he phoned Raina. She picked up on the third ring.

"Akis? I'm glad you phoned. We were all worried. Is everything okay?"

How strange what a piece of news could do to change everything. She was no longer a mystery in his eyes and the tone in her voice reflected genuine anxiety. The fact that he'd doubted her and had assumed she had an agenda, shamed him. It caused him to wonder how many women he'd falsely labeled when they were as innocent as Raina.

"That all depends on you." He gripped the phone tighter.

"So…there was no emergency with your business, or—or your brother?" Her voice sounded shaky.

Touched by her concern he said, "No. The problem was a power-grid failure that was soon put to right." This emergency was one closer to home. One so serious, he could hardly breathe. "I'm on my way over to talk to you."

"No, Akis. I've gone to bed."

"Then I'll see you tomorrow. We'll do whatever we feel like. I promise not to touch you unless you want me to. I've never met a woman remotely like you. I want to get to know you better, Raina. It would be worth everything to me."

Silence met his question.

"I'm not a god. As you found out in the pool, I'm a mortal with flaws trying to make it through this life. By a stroke of fate you were at the reception when I needed a woman who would dance with me. I haven't been the same since you lifted those violet eyes to me and told me you didn't speak Greek."

"I lied," she murmured. "I know about ten words."

His eyes closed tightly. "If you want nothing more to do with me, then say no in Greek and I'll leave you alone." It would serve him right. He didn't deserve her attention. He held the phone so tightly while he waited, it was amazing it didn't break.

"Neh," he heard her say.

"That means yes, not no."

"I know. I'll be here in the morning when you come over. I admit I'd like to get to know you better, even if it goes against my better judgment. Good night."

An honest woman.

Akis released the breath he was holding. *"Kalineekta, thespinis."*

Raina spent a restless night waiting for morning to come. After hearing from Akis last night, she'd had trouble getting to sleep. She turned on television just as the news came on. All of a sudden she saw herself and Akis leaving the Grand Bretagne to get into the limo. It was already old news, but still playing because he was so gorgeous.

She shut off the TV, but couldn't shut out the memory of their kiss in the pool. When Akis had called her, she'd sensed a change in him. That edge in his voice had gone. There was a new earnestness in the way he spoke that compelled her to give in. Not only for his reasons, but for her own.

Besides his exceptional male beauty and the desire he'd aroused in her, she'd never met such a dynamic man. He'd gone to great lengths to entertain her while she had to stay off her leg. Only a resourceful person would give her a tour of Athens through a telescope and a sightseeing tour by helicopter, making sure she was comfortable.

He'd been generous with his time and was obviously successful in business with his brother. If she didn't know anything else about him, she knew that much. Chloe's parents seemed very fond of him. When it came right down to it, the big problem was the fact that he was Greek and lived here. Before long she had to go home.

But until that day came, she had to admit to a growing excitement at spending time with him. She couldn't remember the last time she'd taken a true vacation. Not since before her marriage to Byron.

Yes, it was taking a big risk to be with Akis, but she was tired of the continual battle to protect her heart. Before her grandfather had died, he'd warned her not to stay closed up because of Byron. She was too young to go through life an old maid because of one wretched man who didn't know the first thing about being a husband.

"Oh, Grandfather—I wish you were here. I've met a man who has stirred me like no other. Maybe he'll hurt me in the end, but I'll hurt more if I don't go with my feelings for him and see what happens."

If she let Byron win, then she was condemning herself to a life without love or children.

Raina had listened to her grandfather's wise counsel, but it wasn't until she'd been with Akis that his words had started to sink in.

Until the other night when he'd taken her back to the hotel, she'd felt old beyond her years, incapable of feeling the joy of falling in love or anything close to it. But being with Akis had made her forget the past and live in the moment for a little while. To date, no other man had been able to accomplish that miracle.

Akis thrilled her. He did. For once, why not go with those feelings? She wasn't about to walk down the aisle with him, but she could have a wonderful time for as long as this vacation lasted.

Without wasting time, she sat on the side of the bed and phoned the Maywood jet propulsion lab in Salinas where she worked. She asked to be put through to Larry.

"Raina! Great to hear from you. Are you back?"

"No. That's why I'm calling. I've decided to stay in Greece for a couple of weeks. Is that going to present any difficulties for you?

I've got my laptop. If you need some problem solving done, I can do it from here."

"No, no. It's about time you took a long vacation. I take it you attended your friend's wedding."

"Yes. It was fabulous." Akis was fabulous.

"You sound different. Happier. That's excellent news."

"It's because I'm having a wonderful time. By the way, I was given a tour of the Ionian Islands in our latest X Jet Explorer. Take it from me, it's a winner in every aspect."

"Wait till I tell everyone! The Giannopoulos Company was our first buyer from Greece. They took delivery of two of them just a month ago."

Raina sprang to her feet in surprise. She'd assumed Akis had chartered a flight through one of the helicopter companies. "Giannopoulos?"

"Yes. Two brothers—like Onassis—who came from nothing and have become billionaires. How did you happen to meet up with them?"

Chloe had never mentioned a word. She'd been too caught up in her wedding arrangements. "Very accidentally," Raina's voice shook as she answered him.

"I've heard they have several thousand stores all over Greece."

Her hand tightened on the phone. *You sprained your ankle in one of them, Raina.*

Stunned by the news, Raina sank back down on the bed. The knowledge that Akis had his own money meant he was the antithesis of Byron, who couldn't make it on his own without living off a woman's money. Her grandfather's shrewd brain was instrumental in making certain Byron's extortion tactics for alimony didn't work.

As for Akis, whether he knew about her background or not, it didn't matter. Finances would never get in the way of her relationship with him. For the first time in her adult life she had no worry in that regard. Akis had his own money and was his own person.

"Thanks for letting me take more time off, Larry." Once she hung up, Raina felt so light-hearted she wanted to whirl around the room, but that wouldn't be a good idea yet. She couldn't risk taking a chance in delaying her recovery.

After getting dressed in a clean pair of

jeans and blouse, she took time with her hair and makeup, wanting to look her best for him. Once ready, she left the bedroom on her crutches and headed out to the patio where the family always gathered for meals.

Her senses came alive to see Akis at the table with Chloe's parents while they ate breakfast. He wore a simple T-shirt and jeans. All she saw was the striking male who'd swept into her world, moving mountains to find out where she was hiding.

Well, maybe not mountains above the sea, she smiled to herself, remembering that he wasn't Poseidon. Right then she discovered him staring at her. The longing in his jet-black eyes told her he wanted her for herself. No other reason. He got to his feet and came round to relieve her of the crutches.

"Good morning, *thespinis.*" His deep voice sent curls of warmth through her body.

"It's a lovely morning," she said as he helped her to sit. The soap tang from his body assailed her with its fresh scent.

Socus smiled at her. "What are your plans for today?"

Her gaze switched to Akis who sat across

from her. "I'm going to leave the decision up to my tour director."

His eyes gleamed over the rim of his coffee cup. "In that case you'll need to pack a bag because we'll be gone for a while. For the first couple of days we'll lounge by the water to give your ankle a good rest. After that we'll do more ambitious things."

"That's good for you to be careful," Nora commented.

"I'll make sure of it." Akis finished his meal. "When you're ready, we'll leave in the helicopter."

Raina took a certain pride in knowing she'd helped on the project that had tested it before it was ready for the market. Who would have dreamed she'd end up with Akis taking her for a tour in one he'd recently purchased for his business?

After eating some yogurt and fruit, she stood up. "I'll just go put some things in a bag."

Akis came around and handed her the crutches. In a few minutes they made their way out of the house to the helicopter pad. It was like *déjà vu,* except that this time Raina knew she and Akis were functioning on a level playing field where all that mattered was their mutual enjoyment of each other.

He helped her on board and propped her leg. Soon the blades were rotating and they were off. Raina hadn't asked where they were going. The thrill of being taken care of by a good man was enough for her to trust in his decision making.

After a minute he turned to her. "We're headed back to Anti Paxos."

"That island must have great significance for you."

"It's home to me when I'm not working. En route we'll fly over Corinth and Patras, old Biblical sites."

"I get gooseflesh just hearing those names. My grandparents took me to Jerusalem years ago. We didn't have time in Greece to see the religious sites. They promised we'd come back, but because of my grandmother's ill health, that promise wasn't realized."

"Then I'm glad you can see some of the ancient Biblical cities from the air."

For the next hour, the sights she saw including the islands of Cephalonia and Lefkada filled her with wonder.

"Do you recognize your birthplace?" he spoke over the mic.

She chuckled. "I thought I was born in Carmel, California."

"Then you've been misled. The goddess Aphrodite was reputed to be born on Lefkada." With his sunglasses on, she couldn't see his eyes, but she imagined they were smiling.

"That put her in easy reach of Poseidon."

"Exactly."

Before long they circled Paxos and still lower over Anti Paxos before the pilot set them down on a stone slab nestled on a hillside of olive trees and vineyards. Through the foliage she could make out a small quaint villa.

Enchanted by the surroundings, she accepted Akis's help as he lifted her to the ground and handed her the crutches. The pilot gave him her suitcase and purse to carry. They both waved to him before Akis led her along a pathway of mosaic and stone lined by a profusion of flowers to the side of the villa.

"What's that wonderful smell?"

"Thyme. It grows wild on the hillside."

The rustic charm and simplicity in this heavenly setting delighted her.

Once inside, she saw that the living room had been carved out of rock. A fireplace dominated that side of the cottage. The vaulted ceiling and beams of the house with its stone walls and arches defied description. Here and there were small framed photos of his family and splashes of color from the odd cushion and ceramics. She felt like she'd arrived in a place where time had stood still.

He opened French doors to the terrace with a table and chairs that looked out over a small, kidney-shaped swimming pool. A cluster of flowers grew at one end. Beyond it shimmered the blue waters of the Ionian in the distance. You couldn't see where the sky met the sea.

She walked to the edge of the grill-work railing. "If I lived here, I wouldn't want to go anywhere else. What a perfect hideaway."

He stood behind her, but he didn't touch her. He'd promised he wouldn't, but the heat from his body created yearnings within her. "I like living in a cottage. It suits my needs."

Unlike the penthouse, this place reflected his personality.

"How old is the original house?"

"Two hundred years more or less. If you

want to use the bathroom, I'll take your bags to the guest room."

"Thank you."

In a few minutes she'd seen the layout of the house. The kitchen and bathroom had been modernized, but everything else remained intact like dwellings from the nineteenth century. She adored the little drop-leaf table and chairs meant for two, built into a wall in the kitchen. On the opposite wall was a door that opened onto steps leading down to the terrace.

A room for the washer and dryer had been built in the middle of the hallway between the two bedrooms. He had everything at his fingertips. She sat in one of the easy chairs and put her crutches down beside her. Akis brought a stool over to rest her leg, then he went to the kitchen and started getting things out of the fridge.

"I'm going to fix our dinner."

"If you'll give me a job, I'll help."

"Don't worry about it today."

"Akis? I don't know if you've heard the story of Goldilocks and the Three Bears, but this cottage reminds me of their adorable house in the forest."

"We Greeks have our own fairy tales. My favorite was the one our father taught me and Vasso about Demetros who lived with his mother in a hut much like this one was once. When I come here to be alone, I'm reminded of it. He fell in love with a golden-haired fairy, but she wasn't happy with him and went away.

"Vasso and I must have heard that story so many times we memorized the words. Demetros would cry for the rest of his life, 'Come back, come back, my fairy wife. Come back, my fairy child. Seeking and searching I spend my life; I wander lone and wild.'"

Strangely touched by the story she asked, "He never found her again?"

"No. She belonged to a fairy kingdom where he couldn't go."

"That's a sad fairy tale."

"Our father was a realist. I believe he wanted us to learn that you shouldn't try to hold on to something that isn't truly yours or you'll end up like Demetros."

That's what Raina had tried to do when she first felt like she was losing Byron, who'd married her for money. It wasn't until the divorce she'd learned he'd been unfaithful even while they were dating.

No wonder their marriage hadn't worked. He thought he could have a wife, plus her money and another life on the side. Byron had belonged to his own secret world and could never be hers. Her choice in men before she'd come to Greece had been flawed.

As she glanced at Theo's best man, she realized she was looking at the best man alive. The knowledge shook her to the foundations. "Your father sounds like a wise man," she murmured. "Tell me about him."

"He came from a very poor family on Paxos." Ah, she was beginning to understand why these islands drew him. "My grandparents and their children, with the exception of my father, were victims of the malaria epidemic that hit thousands of Greek villages at the time. By the early nineteen-sixties it was eradicated, but too late for them."

"But your father didn't contract the disease?"

"No. Sometimes it missed someone in a family. A poor fisherman living in a tiny hut in Loggos, who'd lost his family, took my father in to help him catch fish they sold at a shop in the marketplace. When he died, he left my father the hut and a rowboat. Papa married a girl who worked in the olive groves. Her family had perished during the epidemic too. They had to scrape for a living any way they could."

"It's hard for me to believe people can live through such hardships, but I know they do. Millions and millions, and somehow they survive."

"According to our papa, our parents were in love and happy."

"The magic ingredients. Mine were in love, too."

He nodded. "First Vasso was born, then I came along eleven months later. But the delivery was too hard on Mama, who was in frail health, and she died."

"Oh, no," Raina cried softly. "To not know your mother... I'm so sorry, Akis. I at least had mine until I was twelve."

Solemn eyes met hers. "But you lost both parents. It seems you and I have that in common."

"But you never even knew her. It breaks my heart. How on earth did you all manage?"

"Our father kept on working to keep us alive

by supplying olives and fish to the shop. When we were five and six years old, we would help him and never attended school on a regular basis. Life was a struggle. It was all we knew.

"The village thought of us as the poor Giannopoulos kids. Most people looked down on us. Then things turned worse when our father was diagnosed with lymphoma and died."

A quiet gasp escaped. "How old were you?"

"Thirteen and fourteen. By then the woman's husband who owned the shop had also died and she needed help. So she let us work in her shop and helped us learn English. She said it was important to cater to the British and American tourists in their language. We studied English from a book when we could."

"You learned English with no formal schooling? That's incredible."

He stared hard at her. "You're talking to a man whose education is sorely lacking in so many areas, I don't even like to think about it."

"I see no lack in you. Anything but."

"Give it time and my inadequacies will be evident in dozens of ways, but I digress.

"While Vasso waited on customers and did jobs the woman's husband had done, I would go fishing and pick olives. Then it would be my turn to spell him off. I don't think we got more than six hours sleep a night for several years."

"No time to play," she mused aloud.

He made an odd sound in his throat. "We didn't know the meaning of the word."

Raina hated to see him do all the work and got up to help him. For the first time she didn't use crutches because the kitchen was so close.

"Careful," he cautioned.

"My ankle doesn't hurt."

"Just do me a favor and sit in the chair at the table. The food is ready. I'll bring everything over so we can eat." He'd cut up fresh melon and made a shrimp salad. Lastly came some rolls and iced tea.

"When did you have time to stock the refrigerator?"

He sat down opposite her. "I pay a boy to do errands for me when I come to the island."

"No housekeeper?"

"I prefer to do the work myself."

"You're a jack-of-all-trades as we say in English."

"What does it mean exactly? Whether you've been aware of it or not, I've been picking up a few expressions from you, but I'll admit I'm not familiar with that one."

"Jack is a common name and it means that you can do everything well. Now that you've given me some idea of your background, I understand why." The minute she said the word, she saw the slightest hint of emotion cause his lips to thin.

Realizing she'd stumbled on to something significant when he already felt vulnerable she said, "Akis? At the pool when I told you to talk to someone of your own kind and background, you thought I was being condescending. Admit it."

"The thought did cross my mind."

"Since I knew nothing about your upbringing until just now, will you believe me when I tell you I only said what I did because—"

"Because you sensed I was extremely attracted and it made you nervous." His dark eyes devoured her as he spoke.

She squirmed on the wooden chair. "You're right. Please go on and finish telling me your life's story. I'm riveted. The food is delicious, by the way."

"Thank you." He leaned forward. "The widow we worked for started to suffer from poor health and gave us more and more responsibility. One day an American came in and told us the place reminded him of the convenience-store chains in America. He said they were all over the country. We looked into it and started to make innovations."

"Like what?"

"To keep the shop open twenty-four hours, which we took turns manning. Besides stocking it with a few other items tourists needed, we let patrons cash checks and provided free delivery for those living or staying nearby. In time we'd saved enough money to buy half the store. When she had to stop working, we bought her out."

"That's amazing! How old were you?"

"I was eighteen. Vasso had turned nineteen and had to serve nine months in the army. While he was gone, I ran things. After he got back, it was my turn for military service. We both served in the peacekeeping forces and undertook the command of Kabul International Airport."

"It's a miracle neither of you was injured, or worse."

He shook his head, dismissing it too fast for her liking. What was it he wasn't prepared to share? "The real miracle was that over-night we started making real money. After the early years when most nights we went to bed hungry, it was literally like manna fall-ing from heaven.

"After selling the hut, we moved to an apartment in Loggos right along the harbor. When the widow died, we purchased the prop-erty and undertook renovations. In time we'd made enough money to buy failing shops of the same type in Gaios and Lakka, the other towns on the island. We patterned them after the chains we'd investigated and called them Alpha/Omega 24."

She looked at him in amazement. "When I think of two brothers who had the will to survive everything and succeed, I'm in abso-lute awe over what you accomplished. How did you end up in Athens?"

"You really want to hear?"

"I can't get enough. Please. You can't stop now."

Not immune to her entreaty, Akis brought some plums to the table for their dessert be-fore he spoke. "When our staff was in place at all three stores and we felt confident enough to leave, we took a ferry to Corfu. From there we flew to Athens, our first commercial plane trip."

"Late bloomers on your way to do big business." The warmth of her smile melted him. "Were you excited?"

"We were so full of our plans for future expansion, not much else registered. Without the backing of an established bank, we didn't have a prayer. After two days we found a shop for sale we wanted to buy and started talking to bankers. We were turned down by everyone."

Her eyes reflected the hue of a lavender field. "Obviously that didn't stop you."

"No. At the last bank on our list we met Theo Chiotis in the loan department. He was working his way up in his family's banking business. Maybe it was because we were all the same age and he could tell we were hungry, or maybe we just caught him on a good day, but he was actually willing to examine the books."

"Bless Theo," she murmured.

Akis nodded. "He asked a lot of questions and went with us to look at the property the next day. As we explained how we would remodel and showed him pictures, he said he would take the matter up with the bank director and get back to us. We had no choice but to return to Paxos and go about our business."

"How long did you have to wait?"

"A week."

"It must have felt like an eternity."

Unable to resist, he covered her hand resting on the table and squeezed it before letting it go. "He told us the bank would give us the loan for the one store. If it turned a profit, they'd consider loaning us more money for other stores in the future. But the loan was contingent on our offering our other stores as collateral."

"Of course. Akis—you had to have been overjoyed!"

He sat back in the chair. "Yes and no. Athens was a big city, not a little village. We had to gamble that Athenians as well as tourists would patronize us. In no time our number four store was up and running. Vasso and I took turns manning it. Literally overnight we started making a profit we hadn't even imagined and we never looked back. We call it our lucky store. Would it interest you to know that's the store where you fell?"

A gentle laugh escaped her lips. "The concierge at the hotel recommended it so I could buy some headache medicine. After spraining my ankle, I didn't think I was so lucky."

"Fate definitely had something in store for us."

"Certainly for you since you and Theo became best friends."

"Theo had the good sense to fall in love with Chloe. If there'd been no Theo, you and I would never have met." Akis didn't even want to think about that possibility. "While I clean up, why don't you go in the living room so you can stretch out on the couch? There's an evening breeze coming in off the terrace."

"What's that other smell besides thyme?"

"It's the woody scent of the maquis growing here mixed with rock rose and laurel."

"I think you've brought me to the Elysian fields where Zeus allowed Homer to live out his days in happiness surrounded by flowers."

Everything she said reminded him that she was highly educated and had seen and done things only experienced by a privileged few. She knew things you only learned from books and academic study. That was part of what made her so desirable. What could he give her in return?

That question burned in his brain as he cleared the table and put things away. "I take it you don't mind being whisked here."

Her mouth curved into a full-bodied smile, filling him with indescribable longings. "Your only problem, Akis Giannopoulos, will be to pry me away when it's time to leave. I love this island where you come to fill your lamp with oil."

The things that came out of that beautiful mouth.

He took a swift breath. "Raina Maywood? Before it's time for bed, it's time I heard the story of *your* life."

CHAPTER FIVE

RAINA GOT UP before he could help her and walked into the other room, but she didn't dare lie down on the couch. The way she was feeling about Akis right now, Raina would ask him to join her and beg him to love her, so she opted for the chair.

He was a man a breed apart from other men in so many vital ways. What an irony that she'd tried to run from him that first night! What if he hadn't pursued her? The thought of never knowing him was like trying to imagine a world without the sun. She waited for him to come in the living room.

When he did, he stretched out on the couch, using the arm for a pillow. After hearing about his beginnings, she felt doubly privileged to be with him like this in his own private sanctuary. He turned his head toward her. "You haven't told me much about your parents."

Somehow Raina knew that question would come first. "I was blissfully happy until they died. Dad was an engineer."

"Your father had the kind of education I would have given anything for. And your mother?"

"She went to college, but became a housewife after I was born. My most vivid memory of her was playing on the beach. We built sand castles and talked about life while my grandmother painted. I was blessed with grandparents who were there for me when my parents died. I don't know how I would have survived otherwise. They brought happiness into my life again, but they knew I was lonely, even though I had friends.

"That's why they said I could have a student from a foreign country come and live with us during my senior year. I don't know how it happened that Chloe was the perfect pick for me. It was so fun helping her with her English. She was an only child, too, so we just clicked from the beginning.

"My parents' house was near my grandparents who lived close to the ocean. We had horses. I grew up riding and loving it. When Chloe came, we rode along the beach and we did a lot of hiking in the Big Sur Mountains. We made all these plans about what we'd do when I went to Greece. But after Chloe left, my grandmother's heart started to act up and I was afraid to leave her."

"I'm sorry," he murmured. "Was it hard to see Chloe go?"

"Yes, but thankfully I had college and became engrossed in my studies."

He turned on his side toward her. "I missed out on that experience a lot of people take for granted." Akis sounded far away just then.

She smiled at him. "You didn't miss anything." Mindful that his impoverished background had made him the slightest bit sensitive, she said, "What you learned growing up was something no professor or textbook could ever teach you. Every student could take lessons from your work ethic alone."

"Thanks, but I don't want to talk about me."

"I'm not patronizing you, Akis."

"I know that. Keep talking. I love to hear about you. What did you study?"

"My father took after his father and his father before him. I guess a little of it rubbed off on me. I did well in math and science so I went to graduate school and studied physics. After that I went to work for the Maywood Corporation at our jet propulsion lab in Salinas, not far from Carmel."

Incredulous, Akis jackknifed into a sitting position. "Where the helicopters Vasso and I bought are manufactured?"

Her eyes lit up in amusement. "My team did work on its sensor system, one that spanned the electromagnetic spectrum using state-of-the-art instrumentation."

He was aghast. "You rode in a helicopter whose electronics you helped design and you never said a word?"

"Maybe I didn't for the same reason you didn't tell me your number-four store was only one of many."

They'd both been gun-shy of revealing themselves. He got it. "I'm so impressed with the work you do, I can hardly believe you've decided to prolong your vacation here."

"If you want to know the truth, I've worried that you've taken your tour director duty too seriously and your brother might feel that you're neglecting business because of me."

After the information Vasso found on Raina, no doubt he was curious about what was going on and had left a message for Akis to call him. But he'd put off returning it because for the first time in his life, a woman filled his world and he couldn't concentrate on anything else.

"It's getting late, Raina. Before we go to bed, what would you like to do tomorrow?"

"Swim in that green water off your private section of beach. It tops anything I've seen in the Caribbean."

"I've never been to the Caribbean." It was yet another reminder of how worlds apart they were in experience. But her observation caused him to expel a satisfied breath. "That can be arranged. There are few cars on the island, but I have a run-down truck parked on the property to get me around if I need it. We'll drive down to the shore line. Getting there would be tricky with your crutches."

"After tomorrow I'm hoping I can throw them away."

"That can't come soon enough for me. I'm living to dance with you at a charming taverna in Loggos without being impaled." Her chuckle excited him. "We'll take the cabin cruiser over."

"Is the hut you were born in still there?"

"Yes. But today it's surrounded by a vine-yard. The vintner uses it to store his tools and such."

"Did that bother you?"

"When Vasso and I found out what was planned, we were happy about it."

"You have amazing resilience." After a pause, "Can we explore one of those caves that glows blue?"

He was prepared to do anything for her. "Whatever your heart desires."

She got to her feet. "You'd better not say that around me. I might just take you up on it because this has been a day of enchantment and I'm borderline addicted already. Good night, Akis."

He watched her fit the crutches under her arms and make her way to the guest room. The urge to carry her to his room brought him to his feet. Needing something constructive to do so he wouldn't follow her, he cleaned up the kitchen, then went out on the terrace to call Vasso. There was no answer. He left the message that he planned to be away from

Athens with Raina for a few days. If there was a problem, let him know.

No sooner had he locked up and headed for his bedroom than the phone rang. He picked up on the second ring. "Vasso?"

"You're on vacation with her now?" Akis heard the incredulity in his voice.

"Yes."

"Where?"

"Anti Paxos."

"You're kidding! What has happened to you?"

Something that had already changed his life, but he couldn't say the words out loud quite yet. "Do you need me back at the office?"

"That's not the point. What's going on? Bottom line."

"I'm still trying to figure things out."

"Has she been honest with you?"

He sucked in his breath. "We're getting there."

"Akis—I'm really worried about you."

He didn't want to listen. "Why?"

"You've never been hurt soul-deep by a woman. The way you feel about her, she could be the first to do damage I don't even want to think about if it doesn't work out."

"You mean like Sofia did to you?"

"Yes, but I was younger then and got over it. I'm warning you to be careful."

"I thought you gave me the green light."

"So I did, but she's not just any woman. Hundreds of people depend on her as CEO. Don't forget she came for the wedding and has to go back."

Akis had forgotten nothing. The fear that she'd be able to walk away from him after their vacation was over would keep him tossing and turning during the nights to come. Once in a while the big brother in Vasso took over.

"What are you really trying to warn me about?"

"You've let her into your life where no other woman has gone. I guess I just don't want to see you get hurt. But don't mind me. Papa told me to look after you before he died. I guess I've forgotten you're a grown man now and can take care of yourself. Forgive me?"

"If you can forgive me for asking for a few more days off."

"What do you think?"

"I know it's asking a lot."

"Akis? Take care."

His brotherly warning had come too late. It had been too late by the time she'd flashed those violet eyes at him on the street.

After swimming for the better part of an idyllic day in aquamarine water so clear and clean you could see everything, Raina walked on white-gold silky sand to the little truck to go back to the villa. Akis had played gently with her, always careful so she wouldn't injure her ankle. He'd honored his promise to maintain his distance to the point she wished he hadn't carried it this far.

Once in the house, she washed her hair in the shower and blow-dried it. She'd picked up some sun and applied a frost lipstick, then donned a white sundress and sandals. All day she'd been waiting for evening. He was taking her to Paxos Island to show her where he'd grown up and worked. She brought her crutches, hopefully for the last time.

They drove to the only harbor on Anti Paxos, where he'd moored their cabin cruiser. In a lightning move he lifted her like a bride and placed her on one of the padded benches. While she put on a life jacket, he untied the ropes. She could hardly take her eyes off him, dressed in a collared navy knit shirt and cream-colored pants outlining his amazing physique.

He started the engine and they backed out of the slip at no-wake speed until they reached open water. Different kinds of boats dotted the marine-blue sea separating the two islands. Akis pointed out landmarks along the coastline till they reached Loggos. The small, quaint town with its horseshoe-shaped waterfront held particular significance for her. This was where Akis and his brother were born.

He found a slip along the harbor and berthed the cruiser. She removed the life jacket before he reached for her and set her down on the dock. Their bodies brushed, ramping up the temperature from a fire that had been burning steadily for days now.

"Here you go." He handed her the crutches. Once she was ready, they began an exploration of the beachfront with its tavernas and shops. He pointed out an apartment above one of the bars. "That was our first place to live after we sold the hut."

"I don't know your language, but I recognize the Alpha/Omega 24 sign up ahead. You lived close to your store."

"That's how we were able to be on duty day and night."

She turned to him. "I've got gooseflesh just being with you where the whole business began. Your number-one store. When you look back at the beginning, can you believe what you've accomplished this far?"

His smile quickened her heartbeat. "Watching your reaction makes it all worth it."

"I want to go inside."

"The interiors are the same, but we've kept the facades of our various stores in keeping with the surroundings."

He was right. Once they stepped over the threshold, it was like entering the shop in Athens. There were several people in summer gear doing some shopping. A middle-aged man and woman beamed when they saw Akis and hurried over to him, giving him a hug, obviously holding him in great esteem.

Akis introduced Raina to the married couple who ran the store. Their gaze fastened on her with unchecked curiosity. They held a long conversation with Akis in Greek. At the very end he shook his head and ushered her back outside.

"What was that all about?"

He stared at her through veiled eyes. "Aside from giving me a rundown about how business was going, they said you were very beautiful like a film star and that we looked beautiful together. They saw the news the other night where I was helping you out of the hotel into the limo. They wanted to know if you were my fiancée."

To be Akis's fiancée would be the ultimate gift after fearing it was all an unattainable dream. Heat filled her cheeks. "It's evident they're fond of you. So am I," her voice throbbed, "and I'm having a wonderful time with you. Where are we going to have dinner? I'm in the mood for fish."

"We'll go to the taverna ahead where you can eat beneath the olive trees. Their appetizers serve as an entire meal."

His choice didn't disappoint her. The waiter brought *mezes* made of octopus, salad, sardines, calamari, shrimp and clams. They feasted until they couldn't eat another bite. He taught her how to say the names of the fish in Greek. It was hilarious because her pronunciation needed help with *gareedes*, the name for shrimp, causing them both to laugh.

"I'm humbled when I realize you picked up English and are fluent in it. You're brilliant, Akis."

"We had to learn it out of necessity, no other reason."

"Those who know your story would call it genius. I lived with Chloe for nine months, but I didn't pick up her language. I'm ashamed to admit I didn't really try. *Your* genius is that you knew what you had to do and you *did* it against all odds."

"But my pronunciation needs help."

"No, it doesn't." She put a hand on his arm without realizing it. "I love the way you speak English. It's so sweet."

His black brows met together. "Sweet?"

"It's part of your unique charisma. There's nothing artificial about you. Never change."

He reached for her hand and kissed the palm. Full of food and so happy, she felt delicious sensations run through her body at the touch of his lips against her skin. She wanted, needed to be close to him.

"Vasso?" a female voice called out, causing Raina to lift her head in the direction of the lovely woman who'd come over to their table. She was probably Raina's age.

Still grasping her hand, Akis turned around to the person who'd interrupted them.

"Akis!" She looked shocked before her gaze strayed to Raina.

At that point he had to let go of her hand and stood up. "Sofia Peri," he said in English, "meet Raina Maywood."

The other woman nodded to Raina.

"Sofia grew up here at the same time with Vasso and me," he explained.

From the other woman's troubled expression, Raina suspected there'd been an uneasy history. "Akis and his brother must look a great deal alike for you to mistake him."

"Yes and no. How is he?"

"Busy running the office while I'm on vacation. How are you and Drako?" His gaze flicked to Raina. "Her husband owns the best fishing business on Paxos."

Sofia averted her eyes. "This has been a good year for us."

"I'm glad to hear it. Nice to see you, Sofia. Give my best to Drako."

"It was nice to meet you, Sofia," Raina chimed in.

Clearly Sofia wanted to prolong the conversation, but Akis had sat down, effectively bringing their meeting to a close. When they were alone once more Raina said, "She's a very pretty woman."

"A very unhappy one," Akis responded. "When Vasso got out of the military he asked her to marry him, but she turned him down because she was looking for a man who could give her all the things she wanted."

Raina read between the lines. "Now that you and your brother have prospered, she's wishing she hadn't turned him down?"

He sat back in the chair and nodded. "From his early teens, Vasso was crazy about her and she him, but she wanted more from life. There was a period when I feared he'd never get over the rejection. But he did."

She let out a sigh. "Thank goodness time has a healing effect."

His eyes searched hers. "You say that like someone who has been hurt."

The subject had come up. Better to get it out of the way now. "I married at twenty when I was young and naive. A writer ten years older than I came to the house to get details about a book he was writing on my grandmother's father, Edwin Moss. My great-grandfather was a seascape artist who's been gaining in popularity.

"Because Byron was older and brilliant, I was too blinded by his attention to realize he only wanted me for what my money could do to support his research and career. He told me he wanted to put off having children for a while."

"You wanted children?"

"More than anything. I didn't understand why he wanted to postpone it until he was trapped in a scandal with a grade-B film starlet from Hollywood and the director with whom she was having an affair. As you can imagine I thanked providence there was no child born to us who would be torn apart."

Akis's striking Greek features hardened.

"In court I learned Byron had been having relations with her before and during my marriage to him. It got ugly before it was over. My grandparents helped me through the ordeal. Without them I don't think I would have made it. Your brother was fortunate enough to be passed over. In the long run he's the winner."

"I couldn't agree more." Akis put some bills

on the table. "Let's get out of here. Back along the shoreline near the dock is an outdoor club for dancing. We'll see how your ankle holds up without the crutches, but the second it starts to hurt, we'll leave."

Twilight had turned the island into a thing of incredible beauty. Between the water and the lights, Raina was caught in its spell. But for the crutches, she would have hung on to him, unable to help herself.

Many of the shops had closed for the night. "Look—your store is full of people. I'm so proud of what you've done I could burst."

"I'm afraid I'm going to burst if I don't get you in my arms soon."

He didn't know the half of it. Soon she could hear live music coming from the club. They played everything from bouzouki to modern, jazz and rock. Some of the people sat around watching the lights of the harbor and the incoming ferry while they enjoyed a cocktail. Other couples had taken to the dance floor.

Akis put her crutches next to her chair and ordered them a local drink. "Come on." He reached for her hand and pulled her onto the floor. "I've waited as long as I can."

So had she. Today she'd been transported to another world and melted in his arms, dying for the legitimate excuse to get as close to him as possible. Her heart thudded so hard, she was certain he could feel it. Their bodies fit and moved as one flesh.

When he wrapped both arms around her to bring her even closer, she linked her arms around his neck and clung to him. The male scent of him combined with the soap he'd used in the shower acted as an aphrodisiac. Raina had no idea how long they'd been fused together when his lips brushed against her hot cheek. "How's your ankle?"

"What ankle?" she murmured back.

She felt his deep sigh. "When I was a young boy, we'd walk past this club on our way home from work every night. For years and years I used to watch the people sitting around drinking and dancing, unable to relate to their lives.

"It took money and leisure time, neither of which I had. A man needed decent clothes and shoes. But more than anything else it took courage I didn't have to walk in here with a woman and feel I was as good as anyone else."

Her eyes closed tightly. She was haunted by what he'd told her. "How long did it take you to realize your own value and bring a woman in here to dance the night away?"

"I never did."

Raina's hands had a mind of their own and slid to his cheeks where she could feel the slight rasp of his hard male jaw. She forced him to look at her, trying to understand. "I'm the first?"

"I've been waiting for the right woman, but the way I'm feeling about you at this moment, I need to get us away from here now. Let's go." She knew how he felt and would have suggested it if he hadn't.

They walked back to the table. He handed her the crutches. After leaving money on the table, they left the club without having tasted their drinks.

The water felt like glass during the ride to Anti Paxos in the cabin cruiser. A sliver of a moon lit up the dark sky. Raina wanted this romantic night to last forever. When he pulled into the slip at the harbor, he turned to her. "How would you like to sleep out on the cruiser tonight?"

"Can we? I'd love it!"

"Tell you what. We'll drive to the house and pack a bag. I'll grab some food and we'll come back. Tomorrow we'll begin a tour of the different islands."

She removed her life jacket. "You're sure you want to do this for me when you've lived here all your life? Won't it be boring for you?"

"Being with you is like seeing everything for the first time because your excitement is contagious."

"This part of Greece is so glorious, I'm speechless, Akis."

"I'm in the same state around you. Come on." He picked her up and carried her to the dock. They reached the truck and drove to the house in record time. At the house she changed out of her sundress and put on her lightweight white sweats. After packing bags and food, they returned to the cruiser. She really was doing fine without the crutches and had never known this kind of happiness before.

Being with Akis made her realize what a pitiful marriage she'd had with Byron, whose selfishness should have warned her she was making a terrible mistake. Theo's best man *was* the best man she'd ever known, and the most generous.

"We'll cruise over to my private beach and lay anchor until morning. The seats go back and make comfortable beds if you want to sleep on deck. Or you can use the bedroom below."

"I want to stay on top and look at the stars." That way they didn't have to be separated.

"Then that's what we'll do."

Euphoria enveloped Raina as they followed the shoreline to his area of the island. After cutting the motor, he dropped anchor. Theirs was the only boat around. He turned on the lights. It felt like they were on their own floating island. When she looked over the side, she could see beneath water so clear it didn't seem real.

She turned around with her elbows on the railing and smiled at him. "I feel enchanted. It's this place. The air's so warm and sweet, and the sky is like velvet."

His gaze swept over her. He'd turned on music and strolled toward her still dressed in the same clothes he'd worn earlier. Akis was so handsome, her mouth went dry. "I want to dance with you again. This time we don't have an audience."

Raina propelled herself into his arms and he swung her around. He murmured words into her hair she didn't understand. "What did you say?"

"That you smell and feel divine." He crushed her against him, running his hands over her back and molding her to him. They slow-danced until she lost track of time. His mouth roved her cheek until she couldn't bear it any longer. Needing his kiss like she needed air, she met his lips with her own. They became lost in a sea of want and desire.

"I could do this with you forever," he whispered against her warm throat. "My father told me it could be like this with the right woman."

She rose up on tiptoe and kissed his face one dashing feature at a time. "In my darkest moment, my grandfather told me the same thing and warned me not to lose hope. He and my grandmother were happily married for sixty-nine years."

Akis smiled down at her. "Imagine that." Twining his fingers with hers, he walked her to the banquette across the rear of the cruiser and pulled her onto his lap. He smoothed some strands of her hair tousled by the breeze. "If I were your great-grandfather, I'd paint you like this and name it Aphrodite by moonlight."

Raina buried her face in his neck. "If Rodin were alive, I'd commission him to sculpt you cavorting in the swells of your Hellenic world. Have you been to Paris?"

"No. But I've seen pictures of *The Kiss*. All the boys on the island liked looking at those kinds of pictures."

"I think everyone does. Do you think Rodin got it right?" she teased.

"As much as he could working with cold marble."

His comment sent a wave of heat through her body as she imagined them the models for the sculptor's famous work.

"You're all warmth." He lowered his head and kissed her until she was lost in rapture. A low moan passed through him. "Raina—I want to eat you up, every last centimeter of you. But if I do that, there won't be anything left for me tomorrow, so I'm giving you a chance to escape me. There's a comfortable bed waiting for you below where I won't be joining you. At least, not tonight."

He helped her off his lap. The last thing she remembered was the black fire of his eyes as he said good-night.

Her legs almost gave way from the blaze of desire she saw burning there and practically stumbled her way to the steps leading down to the galley. She was still out of breath when she finally climbed under the covers. Akis was the one who had the incredible self-control she lacked. Hers had deserted her the first time he'd taken her in his arms.

The frightening realization had come to her that to know his possession would change her life forever.

Forever...

Akis was a male force no woman could resist. There was no one else like him.

As Akis had done many times before, he slept on the top deck of the cruiser. But he couldn't sleep yet. When his father had talked about meeting the right woman he'd said, "Akis? You're only in your teens and you'll meet a lot of women before you're grown up. When you find *the* one, you must treat her like a queen.

"Your mother was my queen. I cherished and respected her from the beginning. She deserved that because not only was she going to be my wife, she was going to be the mother of our children."

There was no question in Akis's mind that at the age of twenty-nine he'd found *the* one. What tormented him was the fear she wouldn't think *he* was the one. How could he possibly measure up to the educated men she worked with and knew? Maybe that was why Vasso had cautioned him to be careful. Because he knew there was a vast chasm of knowledge separating Akis from Raina.

But when he awakened that morning, he felt the sun's warm rays on his face chasing away the disturbing fears that had come during the night. A burst of excitement radiated through him knowing Raina was only as far away as the bedroom below.

After he'd made breakfast in the galley, he called to her. He'd taken a swim first and was still dressed in his trunks. And needing a shave. She appeared minutes later looking a knockout in leaf-green shorts and a sleeveless white top. Those amazing lavender eyes smiled at him.

"I'm glad you're up, Raina. How are you feeling?"

"Fantastic. Something smells marvelous."

"It's the coffee." But she'd just come from the shower and brought her own intoxicating scent with her. "How's the ankle?"

"I've forgotten about it."

"Good. Come and sit down." He'd made eggs and put out fruit and pastries. "After we eat, I'll take us to Lefkada Island, your birthplace."

She chuckled and sat down in one of the pullout seats beneath the table. "Didn't we pass over it?"

He nodded. "Katsiki Beach will be a sight you won't forget. We'll swim to our heart's content."

She munched on a pastry and sipped her coffee. "I know I'm still dreaming and pray I never wake up."

"I'll do my best to ensure that doesn't happen."

Raina's expression turned serious. "You've been so good to me and have done all the work. I don't begin to know how to repay you. I've never been waited on like this in my life, but have done nothing to deserve it. Before our vacation is over I intend to wait on you."

"We'll take turns."

"While you pull up the anchor and get us underway, I'll start now by cleaning up the kitchen."

He walked around and kissed her luscious mouth. "See you on top in a few minutes." This was happiness in a new dimension. To make it last presented the challenge. If he wanted the prize, it meant not making mistakes along the way. Vasso's words still rang in his ears. *Slow down.*

Once he'd pulled on a clean T-shirt from his bag in the bathroom, he bounded up the steps to the deck and got everything ready. Raina appeared a few minutes later with a couple of beach towels and sunscreen. Beneath her beach robe he glimpsed the mold of her lovely body wearing her orange bikini and had to keep himself from staring.

"You'll need to put this on." He handed her the life jacket.

"Even if you swim like a fish, you have to wear one, too."

He flashed her a smile. "Tell you what. For

you, I'll wear a belt." He opened a locker and pulled one out.

"Put it on, please."

"Nag, nag."

"Your command of English is remarkable."

"I heard the word enough times when an American husband and wife came in the store. His wife would tell him what she wanted and he'd walk around muttering the word under his breath."

Raina laughed so hard, her whole body shook. "Welcome to the US."

His black brows lifted. "I'm afraid it's the same here."

She nodded her head, drawing his attention to the gleaming red and gold strands of her hair in the sunlight. "Certain things between men and women will never change no matter the nationality."

"Like getting into each other's space until there's no air between them."

Raina had a tendency to blush. To avoid commenting, she poured the sunscreen on her hands to apply to her face and arms. "Would you like some?"

"Thanks, but my skin doesn't look like fine porcelain."

Her eyes traveled over his face. "You're right. You have an olive complexion that highlights your black hair and makes you… drop-dead gorgeous." She put the sunscreen on the seat.

His brows furrowed. "Drop-dead?"

"It's an American expression for a man who's so attractive, a woman could drop dead from a heart attack just looking at him. And there's another expression women use. They say 'he's jaw-dropping gorgeous.'" She touched his unshaven jaw with her left hand. "You know. Sometimes when you see something incredible and your mouth opens in shock?"

Studying the curving lines of her mouth almost gave *him* a heart attack. "You mean the way mine did when you looked up at me on the sidewalk? Does an American man say 'she's jaw-dropping gorgeous'?"

An impish twinkle lit up her eyes. "The phrase can be used to describe a woman or a man. And there's another more modern expression. 'He's hot.'"

"Which also works for a female. I've heard that one. Thank you for the vocabulary lesson. I'm indebted to you." But no matter how hard he could try to catch up to her intellectual level, he would never succeed.

"Maybe you can teach me some Greek, but I know it's a very difficult language to learn."

"You mean right now?"

"If you're willing."

"Then you'll have to sit close to me while I steer the boat."

She shot him a side glance. "How close?"

He gripped her hand and pulled her over to the captain's seat. After sitting down, he patted his leg. "Right here."

"Akis—" She chuckled. "You won't be able to drive."

"Try me."

As she perched on his leg, he grabbed her around the waist. "The first word I want to teach you is the most important. If you never learn another one, it won't matter." He started the engine and they skimmed across the water.

"What is it?"

"Repeat after me. *S'agapo.*"

She said it several times until she got the intonation just right. "How am I doing?"

"That was perfect."

"What does it mean?"

"Say it to Nora and Socus and surprise them. By their reaction you'll know what it means."

"S'agapo. S'agapo." She kissed his cheek and slid off his leg. "You're a terrific teacher, but you need to concentrate on your driving. We've been going around in circles," she teased.

"That's what you've done to me," he quipped back. "You have me staggering all over the place in a dazed condition."

"Then I'm going to leave you alone until we get to that beach you told me about."

"And then?"

"What do you mean?"

"You can't leave me hanging like that. Once we've arrived at our destination, I want to know what you propose to do to me."

She let out a devilish chuckle. "I'm considering several options, all of which require your complete attention."

The way Akis was feeling right now, they weren't going to make it another ten yards. "Shall we forget going anywhere and head back to my beach?"

Her smile filled all the lonely places inside him. "What kind of a tour director are you?"

"I can't help it if my first passenger surpasses any sight I could show her. If you don't believe me, just watch the way men look at you when you walk by. I'm the envy of every male."

She rested her head against the seat, soaking up the sun. "Women do the same thing when they see you."

"I'm talking about you. Did you know the newspapers have printed photos of us leaving the Grand Bretagne? The headlines read, 'Who was the beautiful mystery woman seen with one of the Giannopoulos brothers?'"

She turned in his direction. "Chloe's wedding made the publicity inevitable. Knowing her like I do, I'm sure she didn't want it. She's the sweetest, kindest girl I've ever known."

"I couldn't agree more. Theo has a similar temperament. They're a perfect match."

"Isn't that wonderful? Tell me more about him."

"He's a vice president of the bank now."

"Good for him, but I want to know why you like him so much."

The more he got to know Raina, the more he realized how extraordinary she was, not only as a woman, but as a human being.

"You're a lot like Theo. You look beyond the surface to the substance of a person."

He could feel her eyes on him. "I'm so glad he saw inside of you and was willing to take a risk for you. That's because you're such a good man."

"He's saved my back more than once."

"In what way?"

"We signed up for the military at the same time and served together."

Raina sat up. "How did you manage that?"

"His father had connections. I couldn't believe it when he was assigned to my unit."

"I take it that's where your friendship flourished."

"In unexpected ways. We grew close as brothers." He would have told her more, but talking about it would touch on a painful subject he didn't want to bring up today. "When he introduced me to Chloe six months ago, I worried she might not be good enough for him. But nothing could have been further from the truth."

Raina's eyes closed for a moment. She was so crazy about Akis, the thought of his breaking her heart caused her to groan.

"I had the same fear when she phoned to

tell me about Theo. I knew her heart from long ago and didn't want any man breaking it. But getting to know you, I'm convinced he must be her equal, otherwise he wouldn't have come to be like family to you. I'm anxious to meet him when they get back from their honeymoon."

He had to clear his throat. "We'll definitely make that happen, but we've got a lot of living to do before then."

She sat back again. "I'm loving all this, but I'm afraid I'm keeping you from your work."

"I'm entitled to a vacation and have covered for Vasso many times."

"I haven't had a real one in years. It sounds like we're a pair of workaholics. But I have to admit work has saved my life since my grandfather passed away."

Akis filled his lungs with the sea air. "What do you say we forget everything and concentrate on having fun. We're coming to one of the most famous beaches in all of Greece."

Raina got up and wandered over to the side. "Those tall green hills are spectacular."

"You can't access them unless you climb up the eighty steep steps descending along the cliff. Your ankle is doing better, but I wouldn't suggest you try that activity for another few weeks."

"It's enough just to cruise around them. I can't get over how crystal clear the water is. Against the golden sand, you think you've arrived in a magical kingdom. I don't see any other people around."

"Without a boat it's difficult access. Most of the tourists come in July and August. For the moment we've got the beach to ourselves. I'll take us in closer. We can swim to the shore, then come back and eat on board."

"I can't wait!"

Neither could he. Akis needed her in his arms. When he'd found the right spot, he dropped anchor. She'd already taken off her life jacket. Soon she'd shed her top and shorts to reveal a bikini-clad body she filled out to perfection. Raina turned a beaming face to him. "See you on shore!"

A second later she climbed over the side and dove in. Now that her ankle had healed, he discovered she swam like a fish and had amazing stamina.

That's when a warning light came on in his mind, holding him back. His father's words came back to him again.

When you find the one, you must treat her like a queen. Your mother was my queen. I cherished and respected her from the beginning. She deserved that because not only was she going to be my wife, she was going to be the mother of our children.

As if in slow motion, he removed his life belt, pulled off his T-shirt and plunged in after her. He could hear her squeals of delight. "The water is so warm! I've lived by the Pacific Ocean all my life, but you always have to get used to the colder temperature. I could stay in this all day! There's no kelp or seaweed. What's below us?"

"Rocks made of soft limestone."

She did a somersault and swam beneath the water. He kept track of her until she emerged further away. "They *are* soft." Her laughter was music to his ears before she started swimming parallel to the long shoreline.

He'd brought her here to spend time with her and love her, but his father's words wouldn't leave him alone.

CHAPTER SIX

RAINA TURNED AROUND and trod water while she watched Akis coming after her like a torpedo at high speed. While his strong arms cleaved the water, his powerful legs kicked up a fountain.

Her heart raced madly as he came to a stop in front of her and raised his dark head. She could never get enough of just looking at him. "I feel like a happy little girl who's finally out of school for the summer and has all day to play."

"Except that you don't look like a little girl. Do you have any conception of what kind of a problem that presents for me?"

The tremor in his voice told her what he was holding back through sheer willpower. 'It's not exactly easy for me, either. I've come out to play with a man."

Lines darkened his features. "How many men have been in your life?"

"You mean ones who were important?"

"Yes."

She might as well get it all said now. "There were two. Before Byron, there was a graduate assistant teaching my math class during my freshman year. He held seminars for the most promising students and has since become a professor at a west coast college."

"What drew you to him?"

They swam around in circles, always facing each other. "His smarts. He had a different way of looking at a problem to solve it. I envied him that gift. He fed my ego by telling me I'd inherited my father's mathematical mind."

"Why didn't that relationship go anywhere?"

"I didn't find out he was married until I'd been dating him for a month."

"Did you sleep with him?"

"No. I was waiting for marriage."

"Raina…" She heard a tortured sound in his voice.

"It was over a long time ago. He didn't wear a wedding ring. At the end of the term

I went to see if my grade had been posted. The head of the math department called me in and asked me if I knew Rod was married. I felt the blood rush to my feet. After I got my second wind, I thanked him for the information."

"What did you do?"

"Rod had a cubicle down the hall. We'd planned to go out to dinner that evening. I dropped in on him. He assumed I wanted to check on the time. I told him to do his wife a favor and take her out to dinner instead. And I added one more thing. I wouldn't be putting in a good word for him at the jet propulsion laboratory. Then I walked out and shut the door. That was the end of it."

A grimace darkened Akis's face.

"I made the same mistake with Byron by putting him on a pedestal. He was a published writer who'd traveled to Europe to do art research for more books. I admired someone so intelligent and well-read. He was older and had knowledge on so many subjects. The fact that he wanted to do my great-grandfather's story was a huge plus.

"We could talk for hours about the art we loved. I thought we'd never run out of things to discuss. What I didn't see was his empty bank account and his proclivity for women he could prey on. Have you heard the expression 'once bitten, twice shy'?"

"No, but I don't need a translation," he stated.

"In my case I was *twice* bitten before I learned the lesson I'd been needing."

"Enough of the past, Raina. Let's swim back to the cruiser and have our picnic."

Relieved to get off the subject of her pathetic naivety, she swam next to him. He paced himself so she could keep up with him. He did everything right. How she loved him!

She *loved* him.

She loved him for who he was, nothing else. Raina could finally say it and not be afraid. She wanted to shout it to the world.

I'm in love with him.

Loving him wasn't a mistake.

When they reached the ladder, he got in the boat first, then helped her up and wrapped her in one of the beach towels. He kissed her on the side of her neck, on her chin and nose, her cheeks, eyelids, earlobes.

Before he reached her mouth she said, "I'm going to fix our lunch while you relax. After we're full, I'll give you a big kiss for dessert." Raina was afraid that if she stayed on deck with him another instant, she'd forget everything else.

"Coward," he whispered against her lips before letting her go.

She hurried down the steps to the bedroom and dressed in another pair of shorts and a top. There was nothing she could do about her hair until she showered later.

In the fridge she found the ingredients to fix a Grecian-style sandwich. She made a fresh pot of coffee and put everything on the table with a couple of oranges. Akis joined her. While they finished off their orange sections, he told her they were going to head to Cape Lefkas, the inhospitable part of the island with cliffs seventy meters high. The lighthouse was built on the old temple of Apollo. From there you could view incredible vistas including Kefallonia Island.

He got up from the seat first and pressed a passionate kiss to her mouth. "That's the sweetest dessert I ever tasted. Save me more because tonight I'll be starving."

Akis could have no idea of the depth of her hunger for him. She didn't know how much longer she could go on without loving him completely. If she did that, then she'd never want to leave him. But what did Akis want?

Her experience with Byron proved to her that living happily ever after with the same person you married didn't necessarily happen. She couldn't bear the thought of a long-term relationship not working out with Akis. For the moment they were in a short-term situation because soon she would have to go back to California and once again take on the weight of her responsibilities.

If he wanted a life with Raina to continue, could a long-distance relationship back and forth from Greece to California work? A week fit in here and another week there throughout the year with months of separation in between?

Raina knew she was getting way ahead of herself, but every second spent with him was condemning her to be fatally in love with him for the rest of her life.

There was one thing Raina refused to do. Become so desperate that she'd marry someone else who came along in the future just to be married and have children. She could meet dozens of men and none of them would ever measure up to Akis. If her grandfather were still alive and could know this bigger-than-life man, he'd understand why Raina would never be able to settle for anyone else.

Her only choice was to spend this precious time with the man she loved and see what happened. *Stop analyzing this to pieces, Raina.*

He wanted to show her *his* Greece, so go with it and let come what may. She'd come to Athens for Chloe's sake and had found joy beyond belief. If it meant that she could only experience it for a little while, then it was worth it. Casting any worries aside, she hurried up on deck and felt two arms grab her from behind.

"It took you long enough. I've been waiting for this." He turned her around and lowered his head, covering her mouth with his own. Once again she was swept away. They'd started devouring each other when Akis unexpectedly lifted his lips from hers. "I can't get enough of you, Raina."

She let out a shaky breath. "I'm in the same condition."

His hands gripped her shoulders. "I thought I could do this, but I can't."

When she saw the torment in his black gaze, she shuddered. "What's wrong?"

With a sound of reluctance, he let go of her. "I'd intended to vacation with you, but it's not working. Do you mind if we go back to the house?"

Raina took a step away from him. "Is it me? Something I've done?"

His answer was a long time in coming. "It's nothing you've done. I want to make love to you more than you can imagine, but I don't have the right."

Afraid her legs wouldn't support her, she found the nearest banquette so she could sit. Filled with anguish, she couldn't look at him. "What are you talking about?"

"You're wonderful, Raina, and you've changed my life to the point I don't know where I am."

She threw her head back. "Since you asked me to dance at the reception, my life hasn't been the same, either. Taking a vacation probably wasn't a good idea, but I'll never regret the time we've spent together. If that's what you want, then by all means let's go back to Anti Paxos."

His face was an expressionless mask. "It

isn't what I want, but I don't see another alternative for our situation."

She didn't know what was driving this latest decision. But if by situation he meant that not making love to her had ruined the trip for him, then she agreed there was no point in prolonging it.

"All right." In a quick move she reached for the life jacket and put it on. "While you get us under way, I'll go below to clean things up in the kitchen and pack."

He didn't try to stop her. After getting the work done, she stayed below the whole time and rested her leg on the bed, knowing he would prefer to be alone. Her pain had gone beyond tears. When he cut the motor, she realized they'd returned to the harbor and was surprised the return trip had been so fast. There was only a slight rocking movement of the boat now that he'd pulled into the slip.

She heard footsteps in the hallway and checked her watch. It was seven-thirty. He peered inside the bedroom with an indecipherable expression in his dark eyes. "I'll take your bag to the truck. Are you ready?"

"Yes." Raina got up and followed him to the deck. "Just a minute. I need to stow the life jacket." Once she'd taken it off and put it under the bench, she reached for the hand he extended to help her onto the dock. She thought he'd let go, but he kept it grasped in the warmth of his until he helped her into the truck in the parking area.

They drove in silence to his villa nestled in the greenery. It already felt like home to her. When it came time to say goodbye to this place, the wrench would be excruciating. She got out with her purse and started ahead of him along the path leading to the house. No longer needing the crutches she'd left behind, she climbed the steps to the back door. Akis let them in.

He walked her to the guest bedroom and put her bag down. "While you freshen up, I'll start dinner." Whatever emotions had been building inside him, he hadn't made her privy to them.

"I won't be long."

She headed for the bathroom to shower and wash her hair. After using a towel to dry it, she put on her sundress. Raina had picked up a lot of sun. Even with the sunscreen, her skin felt tender. The straps of the dress wouldn't hurt so much.

Once she'd brushed her hair, she put on lipstick and felt ready to face Akis. Before the night was over she knew there'd be a conversation and she was dreading it. When she walked into the living room, she saw that he'd opened the terrace doors. The table had been set on the patio.

He flicked her a glance and told her to come and eat. Akis had put another salad together along with fruit, rolls and coffee. He helped her into her chair and took a seat opposite her. "You picked up a lot of sun today."

"I know. I'm feeling it now."

"Skin like yours needs special care."

Don't keep it up, Akis. I can't take it.

She'd lost her appetite, but ate a little of everything so she wouldn't offend him. "Thank you for taking me to Lefkada. I loved every minute of it, including the helicopter tours."

He eyed her over the rim of his coffee cup. "Do you still remember the word I taught you?"

"*S'agapo.* I promise to try it out on Chloe's parents as soon as we fly back." When there was no response, Raina got to her feet. She couldn't stand their stilted, unnatural conversation. "Since we're both through eating, I'll clear the table. I can't tell you how nice it is to be able to walk around without crutches."

"I can only imagine."

After two trips to the kitchen, she returned to the terrace, breathing in the fragrant air. It filtered through the house, arousing her senses. This was all too much. "If you'll excuse me, I'm going to phone Nora. I promised her I'd call her, but I forgot last night. I don't want her worried."

Akis had gotten to his feet. "Don't take too long. After you've assured her you're all right, come back to the living room. I want you with me. We need to talk."

He wanted her with him? She didn't understand him. Her heightened pulse rate refused to go back to normal. "Nora may not even be available. If not, I'll leave a message."

As it turned out, the call went through to the Milonises' voice messaging. She told them Akis had brought her to Anti Paxos and they'd been out in the cruiser to Lefkada. After saying she'd see them soon, she hung up and returned to the semidark living room. Akis was still out on the terrace.

His arms were stretched out against the

railing, presenting a hard muscled silhouette against the starry sky.

"Akis?" she called quietly from the doorway.

He turned so he was facing her. "I made a promise to you before we flew here. But today I was so terrified I was going to break it, I had to do something to stop myself. The only thing I could think of was to bring you back here while I got myself under control."

She swallowed hard. "Did it occur to you that I wanted you to break it?"

"Yes," he said in a gravelly voice. "But I don't think you know what you're saying. If I touch you, I won't be able to stop. I want you so badly, I'm trembling. I thought I could vacation with you and handle it, but it isn't possible to control what I'm feeling. Tomorrow I'll take you back to Chloe's."

Her heart rebelled at his words. "What are you afraid of?"

"I don't want an affair with you and then have to say goodbye."

Raina could hardly breathe. "Why does it have to be an affair?"

"Because I want to make love to you. But you're the kind of woman a man wants to marry before he takes her to bed."

"And you don't want marriage because you prefer to remain a bachelor. Is that what you're saying?"

His chest rose and fell visibly. "More to the point, you wouldn't want to marry me. I could never be your equal."

"Why would you say something like that? I know we haven't known each other long. But if you feel as strongly about me as I do you, what is there to prevent us from marrying? Is there some dark secret you've been hiding?"

His hand went to the back of his neck. "Not a secret, but I'm not marriage material for a woman like you."

A slight gasp of pain escaped her lips because he'd delivered the words with a chilling finality. "What do you mean a woman like me? If this is your unique way of letting me know up front that marriage isn't in your future, I get the message. You're the one who brought it up, not me."

"After the pain your ex-husband put you through, I'm trying to be totally honest with you."

"Except you haven't told me why you're not marriage material. What am I to think about a cryptic comment like that?" Her anger flared.

"However honorable you're trying to be, you have no clue about what I'm thinking or what drives me."

He moved closer until she could see his black eyes glittering. "I know a lot more about you than you think. You're the gorgeous young heiress to the Maywood fortune, the darling of the paparazzi from coast to coast. The Maywood estate in Carmel is one of the wonders of your state. Your corporation is one that helps keep the economy of California afloat. Your philanthropic projects are well known."

His admission stunned her so much she couldn't talk.

"According to the newspapers, besides your important work at its jet-propulsion laboratory, you run the entire corporation like a captain runs his ship, involved in every aspect. I happen to know that the Maywood tactical defense-system group works on air-defense issues, particularly air-vehicle survivability where the vulnerability of the US Air Force is concerned. Do I need to go on?"

By now her body was trembling. "So you've done your homework on me. I guess that means Chloe didn't keep her promise to me after all." The knowledge stung.

His expression grew fierce. "What promise?"

"That she wouldn't tell her husband-to-be that her old scandal-plagued heiress friend was coming to Greece. Did you know she'd asked me to be her maid of honor? Much as I would have loved to do that, I told her it wouldn't work. It was her special day. I didn't want my being there with all my baggage to ruin it for her. That's why she chose Althea."

Akis shook his head. "Neither Chloe nor Theo said anything to me. You've got this all wrong."

"Then how did you find out about me? No one was supposed to know I was coming. In order to keep the press from creating chaos at her wedding and swarming around me instead of focusing on her at the church, I chose to slip into Greece unnoticed.

"Out of consideration for her I flew on a commercial airline and stayed in a budget hotel in order not to be recognized. We agreed that I'd attend the reception as one of the guests. She made sure that there would be a place for me to sit at one of the tables in the rear of the ballroom while I watched."

"I believe you, Raina. Now you need to listen to me. I found out about you from a completely difference source."

"What source would that be?" Her voice sounded shrill, even to her own ears. "It's finally making sense that you singled me out for a dance in the ballroom. I honestly believed it was pure accident that we met. You were the best man and as such, *you* took on the job of entertaining me. I can hear the conversation now."

"Stop, Raina. It was my brother who told me about you."

She blinked in shock. "What do you mean, your brother?"

"He knew I had a lot of questions about you and he did some digging without my permission."

Adrenaline filled her system. "You two really do watch out for each other. What happened? When he found out my secrets and told you, did you decide to give me a thrill and ask me to dance?

"Was it because I'd had such a bad time of it with that awful husband of mine, you took pity on me? I was so vulnerable, you knew I wouldn't turn down the best man. And once again I was so desperate for attention, I bought it. No matter what I said or did, you kept coming and refused to be put off."

"If you'll let me explain—"

"Explain what?" She was borderline hysterical. "For the first time in my life I thought, here's a man who wants to get to know me better, just for me and no other reason! What a joke!

"You have no idea what a heady experience it was to see you barge in on Chloe's parents looking for me." Tears trickled down her hot cheeks. "Here I thought something extraordinary had happened that night. But all along you put on an exhibition that rivaled anything Poseidon could have done with all his power."

"*Raina*—"

"I have to hand it to you, Kyrie Giannopoulos." She kept on talking, too fired up to stop. "All this time you've been toying with me, shoring me up while I was in Greece because I was a pathetic mess. But it shook you up when I brought up the *m* word. That idea became too real to you."

"You don't know what you're talking about."

"No? Who better to take on the responsibility than the best man Akis? My sprained ankle gave you the perfect excuse to see to my comfort, but you played your part too well and it has rebounded on you."

She was running out of breath. "Let me tell you something. I never want to be someone's project." The tears were gushing now, but she didn't care. "I suppose I should be grateful to your brother. It's taught me there's absolutely no one in this world I can trust. For the first time in his life, my grandfather was wrong."

"Don't say anymore," he whispered from lips that looked as pale as his face.

"I won't. I'm through and am ready to leave."

"Agape mou—"

But she was too far gone to acknowledge his cry that came out in Greek. "Tomorrow I'll go back to Chloe's. You can remain here and you won't have to lift a finger for me. You've done more than enough. Who could have been more qualified than a Giannopoulos to carry the water without complaint?

"In case you don't understand the expression, it means you took on the job of giving this old maid a thrill out of the kindness of your heart. Congratulations to you and your brother who've gotten everything you want out of life, yet can still throw a few crumbs to those less fortunate."

Akis stood there dumbfounded while she ran down the hall to the guest room and shut the door. Because of his fear that he didn't have the credentials to be the kind of husband she deserved, he was afraid to propose marriage to her. But he'd handled this all wrong and had said things that had turned the most heavenly day of his life into a nightmare.

He couldn't let another minute go by allowing her to believe the worst about him. This was all his fault and he had to make it right no matter the cost.

As he walked down the hall, he could hear gut-wrenching sobs. The sound tore him apart. He rapped on the door. "Raina? I need to talk to you."

She refused to answer. He couldn't blame her, but there was no way he was going to let this go without her knowing the truth. Relieved that he'd never had the door fitted with a lock, he opened it and stepped inside.

Raina lay across the bed with her face buried in her arms, still dressed in the white sundress. Her body shook with tears that tortured him. He stole across the room and half lay on the bed facing her. Acting on instinct he slid a hand into her glossy hair.

"You've said a lot of things and I heard you out. Now it's my turn."

"You don't get a turn. Please leave me alone."

He smiled despite his pain. "I can't do that. You're going to have to listen to me even if you don't want to. Trying to peel away the layers of misunderstanding is going to take some time. But before we start over, there's one matter I need to clear up right now.

"Whatever secret you asked Chloe to keep, I swear to you she kept it so well that Theo never breathed a word of anything to me. Furthermore I didn't know of your existence until I arrived at Nora and Socus's house. They told me the beautiful woman with the sprained ankle I was looking for was Chloe's friend from America and that you were going to stay with them for a while."

He waited for a response. When it didn't come he said, "Did you hear what I just said? You'll have to take my word for it that everything going on with you and me was purely accidental."

In a surprise move she rolled onto her back with a tear-blotched face, forcing his hand to slide from her hair. "If that's true, then when did your brother manage to tell you all about my life?"

"Not until the next night when Vasso phoned about the downed power grid. He told me he'd left some papers for me at the penthouse I should look at before I left on vacation. But he didn't explain the nature of them. I had to leave you when it was the last thing I wanted to do.

"You have to understand he's the older brother and has always had this thing about looking out for me. After I told him I'd met this amazing woman, it made him nervous because I've never been this taken with a woman in my life. He realized how important you were to me already. When he connected the Maywood name with our helicopter purchase, he searched the internet and wanted me to see what he'd found."

She groaned. "I can't get away from the notoriety no matter what I do."

"You did with me. What thrilled me was that you didn't know anything about me, either.

"In a world that worships money, Vasso and I are constantly stalked by the press. Their voracious hunger to pry into our lives has been a nightmare.

"Don't you see, Raina? For once in our lives, you and I were simply two ordinary people who met by accident and were seized by an attraction we couldn't control or dismiss."

Raina gazed at him in the semidarkness with her soul in those violet eyes. "To be fair, I discovered who you were in a round-about way. When I called the lab to tell them I was going to prolong my vacation, I inadvertently informed Larry that I'd just ridden in our newest model helicopter and that it performed beautifully.

"That's when he told me that the famous rags-to-riches billionaire Giannopoulos brothers were the first from Greece to purchase them. Suddenly everything made sense...the Giannopoulos Complex and penthouse, this house set on property only people with great wealth can afford, a state-of-the-art cabin cruiser."

He put his arm around her and pulled her

close. "You never said a word," he murmured against her lips.

"Neither did you."

"I didn't want anything to ruin our relationship."

"Neither did I."

He cupped her face in his hands. "Except for the last few minutes in the living room, I've never been happier in my life."

"Akis—" She moaned his name before he couldn't stand it any longer and plundered her mouth over and over again. She met him with an avid eagerness he could only dream about. For the next while they communed in the most primal way. Time passed as they bestowed kiss after kiss on each other until he was held in the thrall of ecstasy.

"You're my heart's desire, Raina," he murmured into the curve of her neck. "But I don't want to make a wrong move with you. No one needs to tell me you're not just any woman. I knew it the second we met."

Out of breath, she lifted her head and rolled away from him. Sitting on the edge of the bed she said, "When I came to Greece, I never imagined something like this happening. I was ready to leave the reception when you asked me to dance. It seemed like some trickery of magic that the best man found his way to my table. I'd watched you all evening.

"But even with all these emotions, I still feel like my happiness is going to be taken from me."

"Why?"

"Because I don't know if your feelings are as intense as mine, that they'll last…"

He got to his feet. "Don't you know I suffer from the same fear? We've both been taken by surprise. I don't want to do anything to ruin it. Before this goes any further, there's something I need to tell you about me that could alter your feelings where I'm concerned."

"In what way?"

"You told me you were hoping to have children after you got married, but children weren't part of your husband's plan."

Exasperated, she stood up. "What does that have to do with our situation? We're not contemplating marriage."

"You have no idea what's on my mind." Did that mean he'd entertained the thought? Her heart skipped a beat because tonight she'd wished he'd been her husband and they were on their honeymoon. "Even so, you deserve to know the truth about me."

She felt a moment of panic. "What truth?"

"I'm simply trying to say that if we were to become intimate, you wouldn't have to worry about getting pregnant."

She hugged her arms to her waist. "Because you wouldn't want children whether in or out of wedlock?"

"I didn't say that. While I was in the military, I came down with mumps. I'm one of the thirteen percent of men who developed mumps-related orchitis. It rendered me sterile."

A quiet gasp escaped. "You weren't vaccinated?"

"Afraid not."

"But that was ten years ago. Today there are any number of specialists in that field. Have you been to one recently?"

"No. I've never had a reason to be worried about it. But after you told me the history with your husband, I know having children means everything to you."

And no doubt to him.

Her heart bled for him. "I'm so sorry, Akis.

Have you had this conversation with the other women in your life?"

"There've only been a few, but the answer is no."

"Why not?"

"Because no woman ever made me want to carry her off where I could get her alone to myself for the duration."

His admission just described her condition, causing her body to quiver in reaction. "I'm touched that you would reveal something so personal to me."

She had to assume that the only reason he'd told her these things was so she wouldn't be expecting a marriage proposal at the end of their vacation. There was always adoption, but he wouldn't want to hear that from her. The painful conversation had gone in a different direction. Needing to change the subject she said, "Where are we going to go exploring tomorrow?"

His head jerked upward. "You've changed your mind about going back to Chloe's?"

"You know why I said it, but if you'd rather I did…"

In the next breath he grasped her upper arms and drew her to him. "You know damn well I want to spend as much time with you as I possibly can until you have to go back to California."

"That's what I want, too." Without conscious thought she pressed her mouth to his, wanting him to know her feelings for him ran deeper than he knew.

He kissed her long and hard before lifting his head. "I'm going to let you go to sleep. Tomorrow over breakfast we'll come up with an itinerary. If there's something you want to do, we'll do it."

CHAPTER SEVEN

IF THERE'S SOMETHING you want to do, we'll do it.

Akis's words went round and round in Raina's head for the rest of the night. He was a conflicted man. On the one hand he didn't want to make love to her because she was the kind of a woman you married first.

On the other hand, Akis seemed convinced that her desire for a baby prevented him from entertaining marriage to her or any woman for that matter. He'd set up an impossible situation where Raina couldn't win.

He'd all but broken down and told her he was in love with her. Every sign was there. If she could penetrate that part of his psyche and make him realize his sterility didn't matter to her in the way he thought...

She would reason with him. Marriage was a risk. How many women got married and then found out that they had a problem that would prevent them from getting pregnant? Those situations happened to thousands of couples.

After moving restlessly for most of the night, an idea came to her and she was able to fall asleep. The next morning she awakened with a firm plan in mind. She freshened up and dressed in shorts and a small print blouse.

Before she'd left California she'd packed a pair of sneakers, but hadn't used them while she'd been here. Glad she was prepared, she put them on, eager to give them a workout today.

As usual, Akis had gotten up ahead of her and had breakfast waiting on the patio. He got up from the chair where he was drinking coffee. "Good morning, *thespinis.*" His eyes played over as he helped her to be seated.

"It's another beautiful morning. Does it ever get cloudy here?"

He smiled. Akis was so attractive, her heart literally jumped. "It rarely rains in June. You've come at the perfect time."

"I'm so lucky, and this looks delicious, as always." She started with eggs and a roll covered with marmalade. "No wonder Chloe chose this month to be married. Where are they going to live? Do you know?"

"They've bought a home in the northwest area of Athens called Marousi."

"I'll bet Chloe is so excited to set up her own house. She has a real eye for decor." Even back in high school her friend had dreamed of being married and having children, but Raina stayed away from that subject.

Akis flicked her a glance. "Have you decided where you'd like to visit today?"

"I have. I'd like us to take the cruiser to Paxos. When we went there before, I had to use crutches. Today I feel like walking and would like to visit all your old haunts like your first home, the school where you went when you had time. How about the home where your mother grew up? Could we visit the church where your parents were married?"

He averted his eyes. "None of it is that exciting."

"Maybe not to you, but I can't think of anything I'd rather do more. Unless it brings back painful memories. Does it?" she asked quietly.

"Not at all, but I supposed you wanted to see some of the other islands like Kefallonia."

"Maybe tomorrow, or another time."

Akis seemed engrossed in thought. While he finished his coffee, she cleared the table, anxious to get underway. This could be the most important day of her life if all went well.

In a few minutes he announced he was ready to leave. She grabbed her purse and left the house with him. "I love this old truck, Akis."

"It has seen a lot of wear transporting baskets of olives to town over the years."

"How did you come by it?"

"I bought it off a farmer who was happy for the money."

She eyed him intently. "Knowing you I bet you paid him ten times what it was worth."

A tiny nerve throbbed at the side of his temple. "What makes you think that?"

"You're a generous person by nature."

"You don't know any such thing."

Why couldn't he accept a compliment? "The way you treat me tells me the important things about you."

He lapsed into silence while they drove to the harbor to take out the boat. Maybe she shouldn't have suggested they travel to Loggos.

Once they reached the dock, she fastened

her life jacket and sat across from him. He started the engine and they were on their way. "Akis? We don't have to go to Paxos if you don't want to."

"It's fine," he said without looking at her.

No, it wasn't, but he was determined to take her there. Raina made up her mind to enjoy this journey back in time with him. She ached to know all the private little things about him that made him the marvelous man he was.

The few framed photos in his house showed his parents, a young, attractive man and woman. There were two baby photos of him and Vasso. Adorable. Her heart pained for the circumstances that had taken their mother's life early. Her eyes filled with tears.

What a great father they'd had. One who'd worked night and day for them and had taught them how to be men. Though she couldn't meet his parents, she yearned to picture their life together. How proud they would be of their sons.

"Raina? Are you all right?"

"Of course."

"I can see tears."

"The sun got in my eyes."

The trip to Loggos didn't take long. This part of the famous island looked like a crown of dark green with jewels studding its base. Akis pulled into a slip to moor the cruiser. She discarded the life jacket and got out to help him tie the ropes to the dock.

She looked up at him, trying not to feast her eyes on him dressed in tan chinos and a dusky-blue crew neck. "Where should we start?"

He'd been studying her features through veiled eyes. "The old hut is on this side of the village, but it's a brief walk by trail. We might as well go there first."

Excitement built up inside her to be exploring his backyard, so to speak. They walked through the lush grove of olive trees interspersed with cypress trees. He'd grown up here, played here. At least he had to have played here a little until he was put to work at five years of age.

Before long they came to a clearing where a vineyard sprawled on the steep hillside before her eyes. She took a deep breath before following him along a path through the grape vines to the hut made of stone. It was even smaller than she had imagined.

Akis! He'd been born right here!

A man working the vineyard called out to him. Akis said something in Greek and a conversation ensued. He turned to Raina. "The owner says we're welcome to go inside."

She was too moved to say words. He opened the wood door and they walked into a stone house with windows and a wood floor. Twenty by thirty feet? There were no partitions, only a lot of vintner equipment and stakes. A counter with a sink was in the other corner.

"This is it, Raina. Our living room was over in that corner, our beds on the other side. That door over there leads to a bathroom of sorts. We had to pump water to fill the old bathtub. The best way for me and Vasso to get clean was to bathe in the sea."

"Were you able to keep any furniture?"

"It wasn't worth it. When the owner took over, he must have gotten rid of it."

A lump lodged in her throat. "Grandpa always said home is where love is. You can't get rid of that."

Akis turned to her and put his hands on her shoulders. He squeezed them, but didn't say anything. They stayed like that until he gave her the sweetest kiss on the mouth. Then he grasped her hand and they went outside.

"We'll climb up the hillside and along the ridge. The church is perched at the top. Because of the foliage you can't see it from here."

He let go of her as they walked through the rest of the vineyard and came to the trail. Pretty soon she saw the glistening white Greek church ahead of them standing alone, small and elegant. Raina looked back to the sea with a sweep of forest-green olive groves running toward it. She'd never seen such scenery.

"What's that white complex in the distance near the water?"

"The Center Vasso and I had built. It's a hospital and convalescent center for people with lymphoma who can't afford that kind of care. All in honor of our father."

"He raised such wonderful sons, he deserves the recognition. Did you go to church all the time?"

"Papa took us when he could."

"When was the last time you came here?"

"Vasso and I come every year and visit our parents' graves on their wedding anniversary

in July. They're buried in the cemetery behind the church."

"If I'd known I would have brought flowers."

"We don't have to worry about that. See all
those yellow flowers growing wild beneath
the olive trees? The broom is in bloom. We'll
pick an armful."

Akis left the path. She followed him and
within a minute they'd picked a huge bunch.
She buried her face in them. "They smell like
vanilla."

He flashed her a white smile. "One of my
favorite scents."

Soon they reached the church and walked
around to the back. He stopped in front of his
parents' headstone filled with Greek writing
and dates. There was an empty can left in the
center. Akis reached for her flowers and put
them with his before lowering their stems into
the can. "There's no water, but they'll stay
beautiful until tomorrow."

She stood still while he remained hunkered
down for a minute. Then he got up and they
walked around to the front of the church.
After the dazzling white outside, Raina had
to take a minute for her eyes to adjust to the

darker interior. It smelled of incense. Akis cupped her elbow and they moved toward the ornate shrine.

"There's no one here."

"The priest lives close by on the outskirts of the village. He'll come toward evening to conduct mass for the workers."

"This church is so lovely and quiet. While you sit, do you mind if I walk around to look at the wall icons?"

He slanted her a glance. "I'll come with you." To her delight he gave her a short history of each one before they walked outside the doors into the sunlight. The rays were so bright, she reached in her purse for her sunglasses.

"Let's head down to the village and have lunch at my favorite taverna. Elpis, the older woman who owns it, knew my parents before I did."

Raina chuckled over his little joke. Deep inside she was filled with new excitement to meet someone with whom he had a past connection. "I bet you're her favorite visitor."

"When Vasso and I were young, she cooked *loukoumades* fresh every day and saved half a dozen for us to eat on the way home from work. She knew we couldn't afford them."

"I love that woman already. What are they?"

"Donuts soaked in honey and cinnamon. She'll serve you one. No one on the island makes them like she does."

Raina was so happy, she was surprised her feet touched the ground as they made their way down to the harbor. He pointed out the school where he and Vasso attended when they could. His life story was incredible.

The second they appeared at the blue-and-white outdoor café she heard a woman call out to Akis and come running. She hugged and kissed him in front of the people sitting at the tables. This woman had done her part for two young boys who'd lost their mother and had to work so hard.

When Akis introduced her to Raina, the older woman with gray in her dark hair eyed her for a minute and spoke in rapid Greek. Raina asked him what she said. His eyes narrowed on her face.

"You are a great beauty."

"That was kind of her."

For the next half hour they were plied with

wonderful food while several tourists took pictures of them. Raina winked at him. "You've been found out. Smile pretty for the camera, Akis."

"Every eye is on you," came his deep voice.

Pretty soon Elpis appeared with a sack for Akis. Raina knew what was in it. "Efharisto," she said to the older woman who kissed her on both cheeks.

"You are his fiancée?"

Raina didn't have to think twice. "I want to be."

A huge smile broke out on her face. "Ahh." She looked at Akis and said something in Greek, poking him in the chest.

After she went back inside he pulled some bills out of his wallet and put them on the table. His black brows lifted. "Are you ready to leave?"

"If I can get up. I ate so much, I'm afraid I'm nailed to the chair."

He came around to help her. By the lack of animation on his face, she couldn't tell if he'd understood the expression or not. The whole time more people were taking pictures of them with their phones. Akis was a celebrity. A lot of people had seen pictures of the Milonis wedding on TV, but he and his brother had been in the news long before that because of what they'd achieved in business.

The sun had grown hotter. When they boarded the cabin cruiser and took off for Anti Paxos, Raina welcomed the breeze on her skin. She stood at the railing all the way to the smaller island, wondering what he thought about her comment to Elpis. It appeared to have caught Akis off guard. That had been her intention. She needed him to know how she felt. But his silence had unnerved her. By the time they'd made it back to his house, she'd started to be afraid.

After setting down her suitcase, he put the sack of donuts on the counter and stared at her. "Do you have any idea what you said to Elpis?" His voice sounded unsteady.

She clung to one of the chair backs. "Yes. I'm in love with you, Akis. I couldn't hold it in any longer. It was evident how deeply Elpis cares for you, and I didn't want her to think that I just sleep with you. If I embarrassed you I'm so sorry," she whispered. "The fault's on me."

He cocked his dark head to the side. "What if I were to take you up on it?" His eyes were slits. "Aren't you afraid I might be your third mistake?"

The question produced a moan from her. "No. For once in my life I know clear through to my soul that you're the real thing." Her voice shook. "The only fear I have is that you don't have that same profound feeling for me. I saw the expression in your eyes when I blurted that I wanted to be your fiancée. I could read it so clearly.

"It was as if you'd said to me, 'Raina? We've been having a heavenly time together, but to take it to the next step is a completely different matter.' Deep in your heart of hearts you yearn to find a woman who's like the woman your father married—someone sweet and innocent with no divorce in her background."

"That's not true!"

"Oh, yes, it is. I understand why your brother was concerned enough to find out what he could about me. Some foreign woman with scandal in her past flies into Athens and disrupts the tenor of your lives. I never had a sibling. But knowing the story of you and Vasso, any woman either of you chooses will impact both your lives because you're family. I envy you that."

He moved closer, putting his hands on his hips in that potent male way. Her heart thudded mercilessly in response. "Let's talk about what I bring to your life. As I told you the night of the reception, my brother and I are in business together. That's the sum total of our existence."

Her eyes misted over. "You bring so much, I don't know where to start."

"Why not start with the obvious. You run an empire."

She shook her head. "*I* don't do anything. My grandfather put people in place who do all the work. Since his death I've been the titular head. If I walked away from it tonight, there wouldn't be as much as a ripple. As for my job in the lab, there are dozens of scientists who'd fill my spot in a heartbeat."

His jaw hardened. "You're telling me you could leave it all behind? Just like that?"

Raina tried to swallow. "That's what I'm telling you. My parents and grandparents are gone. There's nothing to hold me." She couldn't control the throb in her voice. "To put it all in the hands of the capable people already in place and come to you would be my greatest joy."

His eyes closed tightly for a moment. "We couldn't even have a baby that could grow up to run the Maywood Corporation one day."

"We could have several babies through adoption who could one day head the Giannopoulos Company. You could call it Giannopoulos and Sons, or Daughters."

A strange, anguished sound came out of him. "I could swear the gods are playing a monstrous trick on me."

Her spirits sank. "In other words, Aphrodite is a monster in disguise."

"No, Raina. Your grandfather left you a legacy you can't ignore."

"I won't ignore it, but you're making an erroneous assumption. The difference between you and me is this... I didn't create the Maywood Corporation with my bare hands. I didn't do one thing to build it from scratch a hundred years ago. I'm a recipient of all the hard work that my great-great-grandfather started. That's all.

"But you and your brother started your company from scratch. You poured blood, sweat and tears into it every day, *all* day for years. It's your monument to your parents who gave you life and a father who taught you what was the most important thing in life."

"So what are you saying?" he ground out.

"That you can't leave your brother to live with me in California. You wouldn't want to and I wouldn't want you to. Furthermore I hate the idea of flying back and forth so we can see each other for a weekend here and there. It would be ludicrous.

"Since I don't want an affair, either, the simple solution is to live here with you for as long as you want me. I'd rather be married to you, but if you can't bring yourself to do that, then I'll be your lover and deal with it. As long as I know where I stand with you, no one else's opinion matters to me."

"It *does* matter." He sounded exasperated.

"Then what you're saying is nothing will fix our problem, so I should plan to go back to California? If that's the case then so be it." She wheeled around and grabbed her suitcase.

"Where are you going?"

"To change into my swimming suit and enjoy your pool. I need to work off the calories from our delicious lunch. Thank you for allowing me a glimpse of your early beginnings. It meant the world to me. Let me know when you're ready to pack in this vacation and get back to work. I can be ready in no time at all."

He followed her down the hall to the bedroom. "Will you stay until Chloe gets back?"

So he *was* anxious to get back to Athens. "Where else?" she said over her shoulder and plopped her suitcase on the bed. "I don't want to disappoint her parents."

"Do you want to leave in the morning? I'll send for the helicopter."

Her back was still to him. "That's entirely up to you." She opened the lid and pulled out her bathing suit.

"Don't be like this, Raina."

She whirled around. "Like what?"

"You're not thinking with your head. No one with a background like yours just walks away from everything because the man she loves lives on another continent."

She drew in a quick breath. "This one does, but you don't know me well enough to understand. If I leave California for good, money will continue to pour into my personal account Grandpa set up for me. Most of that money will be used to do research for a cure for stomach cancer and heart disease.

"As for everything else, I'll be available over the phone whenever one of the heads of the various departments wants to discuss a problem. I'll step down as CEO but remain on the board. If there's a vote to be cast that requires my physical presence, then I'll fly over. That's it. Not at all complicated."

He stood in the doorway unconsciously forming his hands into fists. "What about the estate? How could you contemplate leaving your home?"

Her chin lifted. "Before I ever heard from Chloe that she was getting married, I'd decided to move to a condo and turn the mansion and estate into a hospital. One wing for heart failure patients and the other for stomach cancer patients who can't afford health care. When I fly back to Carmel, I'll get the process going."

"You'd get rid of everything and live in a condo?" He was clearly incredulous.

"I already told my grandpa what I was going to do when he was gone. He gave me his blessing. I don't need an estate. To live one day in every room would take me a year."

She hoped he'd laugh, but his expression was inscrutable. "Look at this villa—it's the perfect size for you. That's why I love it so much. When you took me to the penthouse, I couldn't see you in it."

"Vasso and I use it out of necessity when we do business and have to stay on site in Athens."

"Ah, that explains it. Where does he live?"

"In a villa about this size on Loggos. But it's a beach house on the other side of the village."

She blinked. "You see? He doesn't need masses of square footage to be happy, either. Why do you think I would be any different?"

"But to come here and live isn't you."

His arguments were getting to her. "Because I'm a lousy linguist? I know I only know twelve words and don't pronounce them well, but I can learn. Just like you learned English!"

"We had to learn it in order for our business to succeed."

"Well, I'll have to learn Greek for marriage to you to be successful. What's the difference?"

"What kind of work would you do here?"

"If you opened up a new store along the harbor here on Anti Paxos, I could help manage it. If you hired another clerk, I could learn Greek from him."

He shook his head. "A job like that isn't for a woman like you."

"Akis—you have a strange idea of who I am. I'm flesh and blood and need work like everyone else. I think it would be fun. Your mom and dad worked together."

"That was different."

"How?"

"Because you're a physicist!"

"That's not the only thing I do. I'm a master scuba diver and could give lessons to people on the island."

"You never told me that," he accused.

"Because it never came up."

"Be serious, Raina. You'd go crazy being stuck here."

"Not if you came home to me at night."

"I can't always be here."

There was an edge of resolution to his delivery. A brittle laugh rose from her lungs like a death cry.

"I'd hoped you would want me here so much that I could convince you. But it hasn't happened, so you win. There's still some daylight left. Why don't you send for your helicopter and we'll fly back to Athens by dark. I'll phone Chloe's parents and alert them."

His lips had thinned to a white line. "Is that what you want?"

"You know what I want, but it doesn't matter. Go ahead and call your pilot. I'll take a swim, but I'll be ready when he arrives. Now if you don't mind, I'd like my privacy to change."

At first she didn't think he was going to leave. She could feel the negative vibes emanating from him. If he didn't go, she was in danger of screaming the house down.

Finally he disappeared and she got ready for her swim. For the next hour she played in the pool and lay back on the lounger. She had no idea what Akis was doing. Until the last second she prayed he hadn't sent for the helicopter. But then she heard the faint sound of rotors and knew it was coming. A stake driven through her heart couldn't have done more damage.

"Raina—you're back!" Chloe's mother clasped her with love and gave her kisses on both cheeks. "You've gotten a lot of sun."

"We've been so many places. It was wonderful." She hooked her arm through Nora's and they walked through the house to the guest bedroom. They'd left Akis and Socus having a private conversation at the helicopter pad.

"I have good news for you."

"What is it?"

"Chloe and Theo are having such a wonderful time, they're going to extend their honeymoon another week. Which means you have to stay with us longer than you'd first thought. She knows you're here and won't hear of your leaving Greece until after they get back."

Raina gave her a hug. "How about this? I'll fly home in the morning to do business. But I'll fly back when Chloe and Theo have arrived and we'll have our reunion."

"You promise?"

"Of course. I plan to leave early in the morning. Since it's getting late, I'm going to go to bed now."

"I'll have breakfast waiting for you before you leave."

"You don't need to do that."

"I want to."

"Thank you, dear Nora." She hugged her

hard, already feeling a loss so excruciating, she didn't know how she would handle it.

After Nora left, Raina got ready for bed. The nightmare flight from the island with a taciturn Akis had pretty well destroyed her. When they'd landed on the pad, he'd helped her down and had whispered goodbye to her.

Just like that he'd let her go from his life. His words about Althea at the reception came back to haunt her. *You saved me from being caught. For that, I'm in your debt.*

"You're welcome," she whispered to the air before she buried her face in the pillow and sobbed.

As soon as the helicopter took off for the penthouse, Akis phoned his brother. Vasso picked up on the third ring. "How's the vacation going?"

"It isn't. Everything's over."

"What do you mean? Where are you?"

"I'm headed for the penthouse."

"I'll meet you there in ten minutes."

Akis hadn't been in the apartment five minutes before his brother arrived, but he'd already poured himself a drink. He held up the glass. "Want to join me?"

"No. You look like hell. Sit down and talk to me."

"There's nothing to say. I just said good-bye to Raina. She's going back to California in the morning."

Vasso sat down next to him. "Why?"

"It won't work."

"What won't work?"

"Us!"

"Doesn't she love you?"

He poured himself another drink. "She says she does."

"So what's the problem?"

"Look at me, Vasso!"

"I'm looking."

"Do you see a man who's worthy of her?"

Vasso's brows knit together. "Worthy— give me a definition."

"I'm not in her league and couldn't be in a hundred years. She's everything I'm not. In time she'll start to notice all that's missing and fall out of love with me. I couldn't handle that, so I let her go tonight." Exploding with pain, Akis got up from the couch. "I've got to go."

"At this time of night?"

"I need to be alone. I'm going to fly back to Anti Paxos."

"I'll come with you."

"No. I release you of the promise you made Papa to watch out for me. It's time I took care of myself."

"Wait—"

"Sorry, bro. I need to be alone."

It wasn't until Raina heard her phone ring in the middle of the night that she realized she'd been asleep.

She came wide awake and grabbed it off the night stand without looking at the caller ID. "Akis?" she cried.

"I'm sorry, Raina. It's Vasso Giannopoulos."

His big brother was phoning her? Her heart ran away with her. She clutched the phone tighter. "What's happened to him? Has there been an accident?"

"Not an accident, but he needs help and you're the only one who can fix this. I know it's three in the morning, but I had to call you. When he left me at the penthouse, he was in the worst state I've ever seen in my life."

"Where is he now?"

"He flew back to Anti Paxos. I heard him mutter something about being afraid you were leaving Greece forever."

She took a deep breath. "I am. I have to be at the airport in three hours to make my plane."

"Then it's true." Vasso's voice sounded a little different than his brother's, but he spoke English in the same endearing way.

"He said goodbye to me earlier when he dropped me off at Chloe's. I took it as final."

After a brief silence he said, "This is my fault for telling him about you. I did it because I wanted him to stop worrying about you. I don't know what has gone on between you two, but I have serious doubts he'll be able to handle it if you leave."

"He told me what you did, but that's not what is wrong. It's a long story. He took me to eat dinner at the taverna Elpis owns. When she asked me if I loved him, I said I wanted to be his fiancée."

"You *what?*"

Raina didn't blame him for being totally shocked. "Don't worry. He shut me down. I think it's because he got mumps and because of his sterility can't give me or any woman a child. He wants to do the honorable thing and give me a chance to marry a man who can."

"I don't believe that's the reason," he bit out, sounding like Akis just then.

"If it isn't, then I don't know what it could be."

"Look, Raina. I don't mean to interfere, but you can't leave yet."

"There's no point in staying. I fought him all day long trying to break him down so he'd really listen to me. That hurts a woman's pride, you know?" Tears crept into her voice.

"His pride is much worse. Do you love him?"

She got to her feet. "I love him to the depth of my soul."

Raina heard a sharp intake of breath. "Then go after him to that place inside of him and wear him down until you get the answer you're looking for."

She bit her lip. "He's given me his answer."

"No. It's a smoke screen for what is really bothering him. Trust me. If you love him like you say you do, don't give up."

"That's asking a lot."

"I'll send a helicopter for you first thing in the morning."

Her nails bit into her palm. "I'm afraid."

"Your fear couldn't be as great as his. He's not as secure as he lets on."

"Why do you say that?"

"Because I've known him longer. And I'm afraid of what will happen if you disappear from his life. I'll have the helicopter there at six whether you decide to take it or not."

He clicked off and left her pacing the floor for what was left of the night. It would mean telling Chloe's parents that she would going to Anti Paxos before she flew back to the States.

For the next two hours she went back and forth deciding what to do. At five o'clock she called to cancel her flight and the limo. When she left the bedroom with her bag, she went straight out to the patio to tell Chloe's parents her plans had changed. Only Nora was up, pouring coffee.

"There you are. I'm still having a hard time letting you go."

"Nora—my plans have changed."

"What do you mean?"

"I've cancelled everything and am going to fly to Anti Paxos to talk to Akis. We had a problem yesterday. In good conscience I can't fly home until we've talked again. Forgive me for making you get up early."

"I was awake." She smiled and gave her a hug. "The path to love is filled with obstacles."

Raina eyed her hesitantly. "Am I that transparent?"

She laughed. "Come on and sit down. As my husband remarked the day Akis came barging out here looking for the woman with the sprained ankle, the second you saw each other, no one else existed but the two of you. It was fascinating really because we'd noticed Akis running from Althea at the reception."

"I know. I felt so sorry for her."

"To our knowledge, Akis has never chased after a woman in his life. Yet the minute he saw you at the table, everything changed in an instant. I wondered when it was going to happen to him. Those two devilishly handsome brothers have been free agents for so long, it's had us worried.

"Their distaste for publicity has caused them to retreat from all the lovely women who'd love to have a relationship with them. But you've been surrounded by publicity, too, so you understand how stifling it can be."

Raina nodded. "I was afraid some member of the press would recognize me at Chloe's wedding and ruin her wedding day. That's why I chose to wait until the reception to make an appearance."

Nora patted her hand. "Chloe told us everything. She's always said you're the sweetest, kindest person she's ever known. Socus and I found that out years ago."

If Nora didn't stop, Raina would be in tears again. "So are all of you."

While she forced herself to eat breakfast for Nora's sake, she heard rotors in the distance. Her heart turned over. Vasso was as good as his word. Maybe he knew something she didn't. At this point she was running on faith and nothing else. He knew Akis better than anyone in the world and he was urging her to go to him.

Socus joined them for breakfast. Nora filled him in before the three of them walked out to the pad with her suitcase. After several hugs, she climbed on board and waved to them before the helicopter whisked her away.

Athens passed beneath her, the Athens she'd seen through the telescope from his penthouse. Tears ran down her cheeks unchecked. She loved him so terribly. What if Vasso was wrong and Akis wanted nothing more to do with her? But Raina couldn't think about it.

CHAPTER EIGHT

AKIS DIDN'T KNOW where to go with his pain. Vasso hadn't been able to help him. For once in their lives the brother he relied on had no answer for him. This was a crisis he had to figure out on his own. Vasso had helped him get to the helicopter at the complex and told the pilot to fly him to Anti Paxos.

When he reached his house, he headed straight for the truck. He didn't care it was dark out. He needed work. It had been his salvation for years. He'd clean the cabin cruiser until he dropped.

Midmorning he grew so tired he staggered down the steps to the cabin. One of Raina's crutches resting against the wall had fallen across the floor, causing him to trip. He collapsed onto the bed so exhausted and emotionally drained he stayed right where he'd fallen. The next thing he knew it was late afternoon. He could tell by the position of the sun through the window slat.

Groaning, he turned on his back. Not since the serious case of mumps that almost killed him had he felt this ill. But it was a different kind of sickness that started in the very core of his being. By now Raina would be flying somewhere over the US to her home of three hundred and sixty-five rooms. He'd gotten rid of her all right. He'd done everything to make certain she'd never come near again.

His stomach growled because it was empty, but he wasn't hungry. He hadn't eaten since their meal at the café yesterday when Raina had told Elpis she wanted to be his fiancée. To be that open and honest in front of the older woman had knocked him sideways. He still hadn't recovered.

When she'd told him she'd be his lover if that's what he wanted, he'd felt shame that he'd been so cruel to her. He'd seen her heart in those fabulous violet eyes. They haunted him now. He looked around the cabin. All he saw was emptiness.

Life without Raina wasn't life.

He couldn't comprehend how he'd gotten through it this far without her. Life would have no meaning if he didn't go after her and beg her forgiveness. Grovel if necessary. It terrified him that she might refuse to see him. She would have every right.

The first thing to do was make arrangements for their company jet to fly to Corfu. He'd leave for the States from there. He pulled out his cell phone and made the call, then he headed to the bathroom for a shower and shave, but he only made it as far as the hallway when he smelled coffee and ham of all things.

Akis had been in a traumatic state last night. His brother must have come to check up on him. Calling out his name he went to the kitchen and came close to having a cardiac arrest.

"Raina—"

She stood at the counter whipping up eggs. Her blond head swerved in his direction. "You look terrible. By the time you've taken a shower, dinner will be ready. I'm fixing you an American breakfast. Did you know breakfast is my favorite meal? I could eat it morning, noon and night."

He rubbed the back of his neck in disbelief that she was really here. "You're supposed to be on your way home."

"Well as you can see, I haven't left Greece yet. Vasso phoned and asked me to peek in on you before I go. He seemed to think you needed help."

Akis couldn't believe it. "Vasso actually phoned you?"

She nodded. "From the look of you, I can see why. Hurry. We're having omelets and they only taste good right out of the skillet. Cooking is another one of my accomplishments."

Raina had so many accomplishments, it staggered him. Still in shock that she was here on the cruiser instead of a jet liner, he showered and shaved in record time. He kept casual clothes on board in the drawer. After dressing in a pair of jeans and a T-shirt, he hurried back to the kitchen, afraid he'd been dreaming and she wouldn't be there.

"You look a little better. Sit down and I'll feed you." She slid the omelets onto two plates with ham and placed them on the table.

"How did you get here?"

"When I saw that the truck was gone, I walked to the harbor and there it was. I climbed on board and found you passed out on the bed. I thought maybe you'd had too much to drink."

"I rarely drink."

"So I went back on deck and walked around the village to buy a few groceries and a pan. You were still asleep when I returned. To pass the time I got busy and made some brownies."

"What are they?"

"A chocolate dessert."

"Now that I think about it, I can smell it. This omelet with the ham is divine, by the way."

"That's because you're hungry. I'll report back to Vasso that your appetite has returned." He watched her get up and put some chocolate squares on a plate before she brought it to the table. "If you're still starving, you can fill up on these."

One bite and he was hooked on them. In no time at all he'd eaten all five.

"They're good, aren't they? The convenience stores carry them. They sell like hotcakes."

"Like hotcakes?"

"Or pancakes. Same thing. Americans love them, but you can never stop with just one. If you sold them in one of your Alpha/Omega

24 stores, you'd be shocked how fast they'd disappear."

"Raina—" He couldn't take anymore. "We need to talk."

"I think we've said it all. Now that some food has brought you back to life, I can leave in good conscience."

"Where do you think you're going?" He got to his feet to bar the way.

"Now that I've made my pit stop for your brother, I'm walking back to the house. Vasso's helicopter is waiting to fly me to Corfu. I'll let him know his worry over you is unfounded and I'll take the plane home from there."

"First you're going to come to the bedroom with me where we'll be more comfortable."

"Oh. Now you've decided I can be your lover? Sorry. I'm taking that offer back."

A grimace broke out on his face. "There's only one reason why I haven't asked you to marry me."

"Because you can't give me a baby. I know."

"That's not it." He picked her up around the hips and set her on the counter. "This is better. Now you're on eye level with me." Akis could feel her trembling. "Look at me, Raina."

"I don't want to."

"I don't blame you. After the way I've treated you, you have every right to despise me. The truth is, I'm not an educated man with diplomas covering my walls. I don't know all the things you know and have learned."

"*That's* the reason you were willing to let me go? Just because some pseudoacademic can talk to me about the differences in Pointillism between Seurat and Signac means absolutely nothing to me!"

"You see? I don't know who they are. I don't know what Pointillism is."

"You think I want to talk to you about that?"

"If we went to a party at one of your friends, they'd see my deficits in a hurry and you'd wish you'd never brought me."

"Oh, Akis—if I took you to one of my parties, the women would fall all over themselves just to hear you speak English with your unforgettable Greek accent. The men would take one look at you knowing they couldn't measure up to you, and they'd be so jealous of your business acumen, they'd croak."

"Croak?"

"Yes. Like a frog."

"Don't tease me, Raina. You're brilliant. I can't do math, I can't speak intelligently about art or literature. I'm not well read and haven't traveled the globe. Chloe and Theo have most everything in common. They suit each other in so many ways. But you and I are poles apart.

"I couldn't take it if we married and you grew bored with me. You told me Byron made a wonderful companion. Even though he betrayed you, he had a cultural background that stimulated you in the beginning. I can't give you that and I'm afraid I'll lose you."

She lifted wet eyes to him. "So you decided to push me away before you gave us a chance to find out what our life could be like? Do you know you could teach a class on Greek history and mythology that would blow everyone's mind? I know your worth, Akis. You know things no one else knows. You can't let that be the thing that keeps us apart!"

He cupped her face in his hands. "I was afraid at first, but no longer. I want to be all things to you. You're my heart's blood. I don't want to take another breath if I can't be with you. I love you, Raina. I love you," he cried against her lips. "I want you for my wife if you'll have me."

"If I'll have you— Oh, Akis..." She launched herself into his arms. He carried her out of the kitchen and down the hall to the bedroom. When he laid her down, she pulled him to her. "I love you, my darling," she murmured over and over again between kisses. "I wish we were already married."

"So do I, but I know a man in high places who can arrange a special license for us tomorrow. We can be married at the church on Paxos. I'll arrange it with the priest."

"You don't want a big wedding?"

"Never. Do you?"

"I did all that once before. What I want is to be your wife and hibernate with you for several months before anyone knows except Chloe's family, and Vasso, of course."

"I owe him for getting you here. How did he manage it?"

"His call at three in the morning got my attention in a hurry, but he didn't have to beg me. The thought of leaving you was so terrible, I doubt I would have gotten on the plane." By this time she'd broken down in tears of joy.

"Don't you know I love our differences? No woman could love you the way I do, Akis. I'm so in love with you, a lifetime won't be enough to show you how much. We were meant to be together, my love."

"I know that," he admitted. "My psyche knew it at the reception. One look into your eyes and the hairs began prickling on the back of my neck. They've never stopped."

"I knew I was crazy about you when you ran to my table in desperation." Their joyous laughter turned into moans of need as their mouths met and clung. Time had no meaning as their legs entwined and they tried without success to appease their unquenchable desire for each other. Akis felt as if he'd been born for this moment.

An all-consuming need to prolong this ecstasy caused him to burn out of control. For the next while he found himself drowning rapturously in her overwhelming response. It was so marvelous to feel this alive, to touch her, love her. She was all warmth and beauty.

But Akis knew that to stay in the bedroom any longer would mean they'd never come out. He relinquished her mouth. "We need to go back to the house and make our plans,

Raina. I want to be married before I make love to you for the first time. My father told me it was the best way to start out a marriage. I'd like to be a good son and honor his final advice to me."

"Then we will, but you're going to have to be the one with the willpower. Mine has deserted me. *S'agapo, Akis.*"

His breath caught. "You know what it means?"

"When you told me it was the most important word I would ever say in Greek, I figured out what it meant and have been dying to try it out on you. How did I do?"

He drew her off the bed and crushed her in his arms, rocking her back and forth. "You sounded like a native just now."

"Then there's hope for me. I plan to learn your difficult language or die in the attempt."

"Don't talk about dying on me," he begged. "Not ever, and not in jest. This is the first day of our new life together. Kiss me one more time before we leave. I need you the way I need our Greek sun to shine. You're my life force, Raina. Do you hear me?" He shook her gently.

"I think you have that turned around. You

swept across the dance floor to my table, and then you swept *me* out of the hotel, crutches and all." She looked into his eyes. "My beloved Poseidon, I'll love you forever. Do you hear me?"

CHAPTER NINE

Six weeks later

RAINA HURRIED INSIDE the villa with all her packages and put them down on the couch in the living room. Before she did anything else, she needed to call Akis and let him know her plans had changed. But she got his voice mail and had to leave a message.

"Darling? I know I told you I'd be at the penthouse when you got back from Crete, but I decided that since it's Friday, I'd rather we spent the weekend at the villa so I'll see you when I see you. Hurry. *S'agapo.*"

She had no idea when he'd hear the message, let alone when he'd be home. It was already ten after five. Between her shock and excitement since her morning appointment at the doctor's office in Athens, she wouldn't be surprised if she were running a temperature.

To get ready for tonight she'd stopped at an internet café to look for the picture she wanted. When she found it, she printed it off. Next, she went to a high-fashion boutique and found the perfect Grecian gown of lilac chiffon that tied over one shoulder.

After running by a florist's shop, she headed for the hair salon near the Grand Bretagne hotel and asked the stylist to make her hair look like the picture on the printout and twine the small lavender flowers in it. From there she went to a shop to buy a dozen vanilla-scented candles. Last but not least, she stopped at a boutique for infants and bought a beautiful baby book, which she had wrapped.

Once her errands were done, she returned to the penthouse and took the helicopter to Anti Paxos.

Time was of the essence. She made his favorite chicken salad with olives and feta cheese and would combine it with crusty rolls and fresh fruit. With the dinner ready, she went out on the patio to set the table. In between the potted plants she placed the candles, and put the last three for a centerpiece. She hid the baby book behind a big clay pot filled with azaleas.

Now to get dressed. After her shower she put on the gown. While she was tying it at the shoulder, her cell rang. Giddy with joy, she reached for it and saw the caller ID. "Darling?" she cried the second she picked up.

"I just got your message. Vasso and I are headed for the island now. You didn't want to go out on the town tonight?"

"Not really. Do you mind?"

"What do you think? If I had my way, we wouldn't go anywhere else."

"I'm glad you feel that way. Are you hungry?"

"Starving."

"How soon do you think you'll be here?"

"Fifteen minutes. You sound like you've missed me."

She was breathless. "I know it's only been two days, but I feel like it's been a month!"

"I'm never going to spend another night away from you. Not having you in bed with me was torture I don't want to live through again."

"Neither do I. Hurry home and be safe." *We have a future awaiting you never thought was possible.*

It took a few minutes for her to light all the candles. The flames flickered in the scented air, sending out their marvelous fragrance Akis said he loved. Twilight had fallen over the island. She'd just lighted the table candles when she heard the blades rotating.

He'd be here any second. She walked to the terrace entrance to wait. In a minute she heard him call out, "Raina? Where are you?"

Taking a deep breath she said, "I'm out on the patio."

Her gorgeous husband appeared in the living room wearing a sport shirt and trousers, but he stopped short of coming any closer. She could see he was almost dumbstruck. Good. That was exactly the reaction she'd hoped for.

His black eyes had a laser-like quality as they examined her from the flowers on her head to the gold slippers on her feet. She saw desire in that all-encompassing gaze and almost fainted.

"You've been away, so I wanted to make your homecoming special. Tonight you're going to stay with me or I'll think you've forsaken me. Come and eat while I serve you. I have a special surprise."

She heard him whisper her name, but he looked absolutely dazed. She loved him so much she could hardly stand it.

"Would you like your surprise first, or later?"

His hand passed over his chest. "I don't think I could handle another one. The way you look tonight standing there like a vision from Mount Olympus, I'm having trouble breathing."

Raina sent him a come-hither smile. "That's more like it. I thought maybe you'd forgotten me."

He started to look nervous. "Is there something wrong?" She could see an anxious expression in his eyes. It was sweet really. Her darling husband was so wonderful, she needed to put him out of his misery.

"Of course not. You're always so generous and take such perfect care of me, can't your lover do something special for you without you worrying?"

His chest rose and fell visibly, evidence that he needed an answer. Afraid to carry this charade any further without an explanation he could live with, she walked over to the flowerpot and pulled out the wrapped package.

"If you'll sit down at the table with me, I'll give this to you."

Instead of the happiness she'd expected, he looked stricken. "It's our six-week anniversary. I planned to give you your gift tonight while we were out to dinner in Athens. But I left it at the penthouse."

"There's plenty of time for you to give it to me. Right now why don't you open yours." She walked over to the table and put the present on top of his plate, then she sat down opposite him.

Akis moved slowly, like he was walking through water. Then he sank down in the chair stiffly and reached for it, but he kept looking at her. Why was he behaving like this? She couldn't understand it.

When he pulled the baby book out of the wrapping, she thought he'd paled, but it was difficult to tell in the candle light. His black brows furrowed. "What kind of a joke is this?"

With that question, she finally understood how much he'd suffered because he thought he could never be a father.

"It's no joke. I've been nauseated every morning for the last week. I asked Chloe to get me in to see her OB this morning in Athens. He took a blood test. I'm pregnant with your baby."

His head reared. He stared at her. "But that's impossible."

"I told my doctor the same thing. He said that mumps for a certain percentage of men cause a drop in their sperm count. But research has come a long way since ten years ago when you came down with them. Since then, he says you've recovered." She put a hand on his arm and squeezed it. "You had to have recovered because I'm pregnant."

When the truth finally sank in, the chair scraped on the tile. He shot out of it and came around to pick her up in his arms, holding her like a bride. "We're going to have a baby! *Raina*—"

He carried her through the house to their bedroom and followed her body down onto the bed. His mouth kissed her so long and hard, she could scarcely breathe. "My precious love." Over and over he kissed every inch of her face and hair. The tie on her shoulder had come undone. She felt moisture on her skin. By now they were both in tears.

"I didn't know it was possible I could be this happy, Akis."

"I still can't believe it." His hand slid down her body to her stomach, sending darts of delight through her. He leaned over to kiss her through the chiffon. "Our baby is inside you."

"Incredible, isn't it. Do you want a boy or a girl?"

"Don't ask me a question like that. I don't care. I only know I want you to take care of yourself. I couldn't bear to lose you."

She hugged his head to her breast, kissing his black hair. "Please don't be afraid for me. I'm not your mother. I won't die after giving birth. I'm strong and in perfect health. The doctor has given me a prescription for nausea. I've had all day to consider names. I can't think of a girl's name yet, but I know what I want if we have a boy."

He lifted his head. His eyes were filled with liquid. "Tell me," he whispered, kissing her mouth.

"Patroklos Giannopoulos after your father. We can call him Klos for short. I looked up his name. It means glory of the father. It's a perfect name to revere the man who fathered you and Vasso."

"It might be a girl," he murmured, kissing her neck to hide the emotions she knew were brimming out of him.

"Of course. But I draw the line at *Phaiax.*"

All of a sudden that delightful, rumbling sound of male laughter poured out of Akis.

He rolled her on top of him. "My adorable Naiad nymph. If we have a daughter, we'll name her Ginger after her earthly great-grandmother who raised you to be the superb woman you are."

"Hmm." Raina drew her finger across his lower lip. "Ginger Giannopoulos. I love it. Almost as much as I love my husband who has given me a priceless gift. Darling—I know what this news means to you. I also know that you and Vasso share everything. Go ahead and call him, then I'll have your whole attention."

A half smile broke the corner of his mouth. "Am I that transparent?"

"It's a beautiful thing to see two brothers so devoted to each other. Your joy will be his. Here. Use my phone." It was lying on the bedside table.

Their conversation was short and so touching, she teared up again. When he hung up, he crushed her in his arms. "Thank God my brother phoned you in the middle of the night."

She clasped him to her. "I know now that Grandpa was inspired when he told me not to close off my heart. He knew something I didn't. I love you so much. I'm the luckiest woman on earth. The doctor says I probably got pregnant on our wedding night."

"Have you told Chloe?"

"No. I simply asked her to give me the name of her OB since I needed a prescription for birth control. I think news like mine should be reserved for the man who's made me the happiest woman in the world."

"We haven't seen them since the wedding. Let's invite them over on Sunday and tell them together."

"I'd love it, but right now I want to concentrate on you. Do you want to eat first?"

"Not yet. I need to inspect my pregnant wife from head to toe."

Heat swept into her cheeks. "You already did when you saw me standing on the patio."

"I'll never forget the sight of you in this gown with those flowers in your hair and the air fragrant with vanilla. But there are other sights meant for me and me alone. Come here to me, Raina."

"I'm here. *S'agapo*, my wonderful, fantastic Akis."

* * * * *

COMING NEXT MONTH FROM

HARLEQUIN

Available August 4, 2015

#4483 RETURN OF THE ITALIAN TYCOON
The Vineyards of Calanetti
by Jennifer Faye
When assistant Kayla travels to Angelo Amatucci's beautiful Tuscan village, she never expected to discover a new, *very* attractive side to her demanding boss... Working together is blissful torture and Kayla can't help but wonder if she'll be promoted...to Mrs. Amatucci!

#4484 HIS UNFORGETTABLE FIANCÉE
by Teresa Carpenter
When Grace Delaney meets a handsome stranger with amnesia, she soon finds herself falling, not for the millionaire he's revealed to be, but for the *man* she's come to know. When Jackson's memory returns, will he forget her...or make her dreams a reality?

#4485 HIRED BY THE BROODING BILLIONAIRE
by Kandy Shepherd
Since losing his wife Declan has adjusted to a life of isolation... But as caring horticulturist Shelley restores order and beauty to his garden, she also begins to thaw Declan's heart. Can he let Shelley's light in and finally have his second chance at love?

#4486 A WILL, A WISH... A PROPOSAL
by Jessica Gilmore
Ellie is living by her rules—not hotshot Max's! But bound together by her godmother's will, their sparks are becoming harder to ignore... Luckily, Ellie makes Max *want* to be a different man and, down on one knee, he'll prove it!

YOU CAN FIND MORE INFORMATION ON UPCOMING HARLEQUIN® TITLES, FREE EXCERPTS AND MORE AT WWW.HARLEQUIN.COM.

HRLPCNM0715

LARGER-PRINT BOOKS!

GET 2 FREE LARGER-PRINT NOVELS PLUS
2 FREE GIFTS!

H HARLEQUIN®

Romance

From the Heart, For the Heart

HRLP15

"Now, if you'll excuse me, I promised to swing by my brother's villa. He wants to show me the latest improvements at the winery." He got to his feet. "Of course, if you'd like to accompany me, you're welcome."

Kayla glanced down at her rather sparse list of notes. "I think my time would be better spent here doing some research."

"You're sure?"

She nodded. "I am. But thank you for the invite."

The truth was she and Angelo were getting along a lot better than they had in the office. She'd been working for him for weeks now and they'd only ever addressed each other with mister and miss, but now they were on a first-name basis. And then there was that kiss…erm, no she wasn't going to think about it. No matter how good it was or how much she wished that he'd kiss her again—

Her thoughts screeched to a halt. Did she want him to kiss her again? She turned to watch his retreating form.

His broad shoulders were evident in the linen suit jacket. His long, powerful legs moved at a swift pace, covering the patio area quickly.

Yes, she did want to be kissed again. Only this time she wanted him to kiss her because he wanted her and not because he was exhausted and stressed after a run-in with his siblings. But that couldn't happen. She needed this job.

A quick fling with her boss beneath the warm sunshine of Tuscany just wasn't worth throwing away her dreams—the rest of her life. No matter how tempting Angelo might be, she just couldn't ruin this opportunity.

And she couldn't return to Paradise as a failure.

Don't miss
RETURN OF THE ITALIAN TYCOON
by Jennifer Faye,
available August 2015 wherever
Harlequin® Romance books and ebooks are sold.

www.Harlequin.com

HREXP0715